The Murail siblings ar ...ors in their own right – Marie ...ude has sold over two million books worldwide, Elvire's very first novel was turned into a film and Lorris is well known for writing about his two passions: good food and science fiction. Together they make a truly formidable literary trio. When writing the Golem series, the siblings wanted not only to recapture the intensity and creativity of playing together as children, but also to write the kinds of books they would have liked when they were young. "It was like a game," says Elvire, the youngest. "It was a huge challenge, but we wanted to lose our individual voices and morph into a new, even better one. It worked so well that sometimes we had trouble remembering who had written what!" Her sister Marie-Aude adds, "It's so important to remember what you were like when you were young. It gets more difficult as you get older – you have to have your own children to get it back again!" It took two years to complete all five Golem books.

Now it is your turn to play…

This book is supported by the French
Ministry for Foreign Affairs, as part of
the Burgess programme headed for
the French Embassy in London by the
Institut Français du Royaume-Uni

Liberté • Égalité • Fraternité
RÉPUBLIQUE FRANÇAISE

Golem
1: Magic Berber

Elvire, Lorris and Marie-Aude Murail

translated by Sarah Adams

WALKER BOOKS
AND SUBSIDIARIES

LONDON · BOSTON · SYDNEY · AUCKLAND

First published 2005 by Walker Books Ltd
87 Vauxhall Walk, London SE11 5HJ

2 4 6 8 10 9 7 5 3 1

Original Edition: *Golem 1 – Magic Berber*
© 2002 Éditions Pocket Jeunesse,
a division of Univers Poche, Paris – France
Translation © 2005 Sarah Adams
Cover image © 2005 Guy McKinley

This book has been typeset in DeadHistory and M Joanna

Printed and bound in Great Britain
by Bookmarque Ltd, Croydon, Surrey

British Library Cataloguing in Publication Data:
a catalogue record for this book
is available from the British Library

ISBN 1-84428-614-2

www.walkerbooks.co.uk

Contents

An Hour's Class with 8D

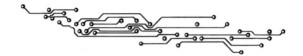

On Monday 6 January Hugh Mullins was getting ready to teach 8D. The young English teacher was newly qualified, and 8D was the most challenging class in Moreland School.

Back in at the deep end, he reflected, emptying his bag. *Year 8 English: Texts and Approaches (A Teacher's Handbook)* weighed a ton. He looked around the empty classroom and sighed nervously. Maybe Samir would be off sick. A loud bellow from the corridor made him jump. Mamadou, aka Motor-mouth, was warming up his vocal chords.

Here we go again, Hugh groaned inwardly, burying his face in his hands. But he pulled himself together when Aisha and Nouria walked in.

"Happy new year, sir!" they giggled.

On second thoughts, the girls in 8D weren't such a lost cause... Hugh wished them a happy new year too, in what he hoped was a formal voice. His more experienced colleagues had warned him, "Don't get too friendly with your students, or they'll eat you alive."

"That's a nice sweater, sir," said Nouria. "Was it from Father Christmas?"

Hugh blushed. It was a present from his mum.

8D always caught him off guard.

The rest of the class arrived in twos and threes, pushing and shoving and shouting. Finally Samir made his entrance. Hugh looked down, took a biro out of his pencil case, opened the register and breathed out slowly, counting one, two, three...

"Sit down please, Samir," he said, without looking up.

Samir always took his time choosing where to sit. According to him, Farida smelt of couscous, Stephen's trainers stank, there wasn't any point copying from Zeinul, and Mamadou would steal your underwear without you noticing.

"Shove over!" Samir plonked himself on top of Farida. "Phwoar! Get a whiff of that, sir. My chair stinks of couscous!"

Everybody sniggered. They were used to Samir's jokes about couscous, the traditional North African dish prepared daily in Farida's home. And Farida was used to defending herself. She started hitting Samir and calling him all sorts of names.

"Sir, my chair's talking!" shouted Samir, leaping up.

Hugh counted to ten in his head, to stay calm. "Samir, if you carry on like this, you'll be through that door before I've even taken the register," he warned.

"No door to go through, sir! The door's on strike, innit? Promise, on Farida's stinky couscous-head."

Everybody laughed, even Farida.

"I'll go on strike too, if you don't shut it!" shouted Hugh, forgetting one: shouting at Samir got you nowhere, and two: threats weren't much better.

"Oh sir, you're scary when you talk like that!" mocked Samir.

Everybody creased up. It was chaos in 8D.

"QUIET, EVERYBODY! Sit down, Samir! Get your books out while I take the register," said Hugh quickly, trying to put out the fire before it spread. "Badach?"

"Here," Majid answered. He felt sorry for their young teacher.

The register was taken without further incident.

Samir produced his Discman. With any luck, Hugh would get quarter of an hour's peace and quiet. He might even make it through the lesson about the transmitter, the receiver and the message, which he'd been putting off since last term. He glanced around the classroom.

Nouria was showing off her new cane-rows to Aisha. Majid was frowning as he read some kind of leaflet. Samir was beating out a rhythm on his desk.

"OK. Today we're going to take a look at the lesson on page twelve in your textbooks," announced Hugh. He didn't sound too convinced. "Nouria, when you're ready…"

Nouria was busy giving Aisha cane-rows too.

"But Aisha *asked* me to," she whined, prodding her friend.

"Geddoff!" objected Aisha.

"Are we having a lesson or what?" Samir interrupted, removing his headphones. "Page twelve, page twelve…" He started flicking through his textbook and reading manically out loud: "'Written and oral forms of communication establish a relationship between the transmitter and the receiver, both of which use a common code to transmit the message…' Sir, sir, get this, they're talking about rap!"

"What d'you mean, they're talking about rap?" Hugh wondered.

"Puff Z Sniddy, he's like an MC with a message, innit? And Onyx FM's the receiver."

"Stop talking rubbish, Samir," Hugh sighed.

The lesson went on with nobody paying much attention and everybody finding something else to do.

"Majid," said Hugh, finally losing his temper, "far be it for me to interrupt your reading, but what *is* that leaflet?"

Majid looked up and gave his teacher a big smile. "It's not a leaflet, sir. I've won a computer."

"Yeah, right," sneered Samir. "Why don't you just shut it?"

"Same to you," said Majid, unfazed. "It's written in this letter, sir. I did the competition in my mum's Price Shrinkers catalogue and I won a computer. At least, I think..." He stood up and waved the piece of paper at his teacher.

"Bring it here," said Hugh, giving up. But when he saw the letter in front of him, he had a flash of inspiration. "Look," he said to 8D, "this is a message. The transmitter is Price Shrinkers. And the receiver is Majid."

"No it's not, it's a computer," Mamadou set him straight.

"Idiot!" Samir snapped. "The teacher, right, is explaining the lesson on page twelve. Go on, sir."

Encouraged, Hugh elaborated. "We're going to study what the message says. Luckily, Price Shrinkers and Majid use a common code – they both speak English."

"You could've told us, Majid!" said Samir.

"Eat your tongue, man, innit!" Mamadou

bellowed from the back of the class.

For a moment, Hugh wondered if his students and Price Shrinkers *did* use the same code, but he carried on all the same.

"So, the letter says: 'Dear Mr Badach…'"

Everybody laughed. Sebastian shook Majid's hand, calling him "dear Mr Badach".

Hugh went on reading: "'We are pleased to inform you that you are the lucky winner of a New Generation BIT computer – the latest in Big Information Technology brought to you by the Big B Corporation. It will be delivered to your home address on confirmation of receipt of this letter.'"

"What's the catch?" bellowed Mamadou.

"There's no catch. As the transmitter, all Majid needs to do is send back a message to the Price Shrinkers catalogue, which in turn becomes the receiver." He looked at Majid, who, for the first time in class, was concentrating so hard it was painful to watch. "You have to write to Price Shrinkers and tell them you've got their letter."

"But … but is it true about the computer?" stammered Majid, not sure whether to relax his guard.

"Every form of communication has a function," answered Hugh, relishing the class's silence. "When the transmitter communicates, he or she has an objective. The function of the communication changes according to the objective…"

The students in 8D listened with their mouths wide open as they swallowed an indigestible chunk of coursework.

"In this particular instance," said Hugh, taking his time, "the function is referential…"

Majid squirmed. "But, sir, what about the computer?"

"We're getting there. The function is referential when the transmitter provides a piece of information. In this instance, the piece of information is as follows…"

And with all the enthusiasm of his twenty-six years, Hugh shouted at the top of his voice: "MAJID'S WON A COMPUTER!"

"RA-AA-AH!" roared the whole class.

We are the champions! chanted Aisha and Nouria, pumping their fists in the air.

"The Badachs'll have to get a plug first," sniped Samir.

"You're just jealous," Hugh teased him.

"Yeah, Samir, teacher's right," said Farida.

"You're *dead* after class."

Just then the bell rang. Majid gave Hugh another big smile. "Thanks, sir!"

He was a nice kid. Actually, they were all nice kids in 8D when you got to know them. Hugh caught Samir glaring at him defiantly. Well, *nearly* all nice kids... He'd heard worrying rumours about Samir hanging out in basements with a crew of older boys from the Moreland Estate. Hugh wondered if they were small-time drug dealers or into handling stolen goods. He needed to get Samir on his own one of these days. But so far he hadn't even been able to get in touch with his parents. You'd think he didn't have any.

Majid did. He had a mum who was round and smiley, with a heart as sweet as the steam from mint tea, and a dad who worked in the markets by day and cleaned offices by night. Mr Badach definitely existed, because he'd given his wife seven sons. But that was almost the only proof Majid had of his existence. Majid was the seventh son.

He was also the shortest and cheekiest.

"Emmay, akli dhe gueham!" he shouted, flinging open the door. *Mum, I'm home.*

Mrs Badach came out of her kitchen, releasing a warm torrent of spices, honey and mint into the living room.

"Majid, you spik Inglish not Berber," she scolded. "Becoz I need learn Inglish proper."

Majid planted a kiss on his mum's cheek. "Mum" in Berber is *yemma*, but he affectionately gave it a backslang spin. He grabbed a moon-shaped piece of shortbread and shouted, "Emmay, we're going to get the computer! My teacher said so."

"Iz good, komputer," Emmay said warmly. "You go top of skool." She laughed, but it was just an excuse to feast her eyes on her son. Majid was the seventh son, the miracle of miracles.

But in Majid's head, the miracle of miracles was the computer…

What About This Computer, Then?

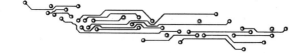

The block where Majid lived on the Moreland Estate was called Hummingbird Tower, aka Couscous City, because all the tenants came from Algeria, Morocco and Tunisia in North Africa. Apart from Aisha, who was from Mali in West Africa.

Any colour and life on the estate was thanks to the tenants, since all the council blocks looked exactly the same. Tall grey slabs of concrete dumped in the middle of what would have been lawns and shrubs, if they hadn't been cut up by football skid marks and mopeds. On the morning of 26 January, everybody was tramping through the mud, including the delivery men from Price Shrinkers.

"There it is," said one of them, pulling his cap down with a disapproving look.

"I hope the lift's working. You won't catch me walking up twelve floors," grumbled another.

There were three Price Shrinkers. They'd been warned that the Moreland Estate was rough and the computer would probably get nicked before they'd rung the Badachs' doorbell.

The ground-floor entrance hall of Hummingbird Tower stank and the walls were covered in graffiti tags. But the lift was working, and the delivery men weren't held at gunpoint before they could ring the Badachs' bell. When Majid opened the door, his whole face lit up. It was a smile of pure joy, and it melted the hearts of at least two of the Price Shrinkers.

"Emmay, it's the computer!"

You'd have thought Majid was announcing a state visit. Mrs Badach rushed out of the kitchen.

"Oh my goodniz, iz for you so big trouble," she babbled when she saw the Price Shrinkers, embarrassed that three men had gone to all this bother for her son. "Pleez to sit … tea iz ready. Majid, roh awid lataye!" She lapsed into Berber as she ordered

Majid to fetch the tea things.

The astounded delivery men had to sit down, drink mint tea, eat honey cakes made specially for them, and then swallow a second cup of mint tea so sweet they nearly choked on it.

"More littel cakez?" Mrs Badach begged them.

The three men were beginning to feel sick.

"No thanks, missus, much obliged…"

"I put littel cakez for childrin, innit?" said Mrs Badach, stuffing almond biscuits into a Big B Stores plastic bag. Then she added some shortbread moons coated in icing sugar. "Back home in Algeria iz called gazelle horn," she explained.

The delivery men were all single, but they left with enough biscuits to feed an army.

"They're quite friendly here, really," said one of them, clambering back into the van. Then he noticed Samir loitering at the entrance to the block. The kid gave him a V-sign before going to pick up a stone.

"Yeah, all right, let's not hang around."

Up on the twelfth floor, Majid was still admiring the packaging.

"You iz not opening it?" asked his surprised mum.

"Shh," said Majid softly.

He was impatient by nature, but right now he felt like he was standing on the threshold of an unknown world. As he rested his hands on the box, Majid was sorry that none of his six brothers were there. They'd all gone their separate ways, far from the Moreland Estate and the dull suburban life of Moreland Town. The eldest, Abdelkarim, was a waiter in a café. Monir, the next, ran a grocery store. The third, Omar, had lost his job at a car factory. The fourth, Haziz, had fallen in with the wrong crew on the Moreland Estate and vanished without trace, to his mother's great shame. Moussa, the fifth brother, helped their uncle run a post office. Brahim, the sixth, who'd dropped out of school and threatened to turn out as badly as Haziz, had been sent back to Algeria on Mr Badach's orders.

Which was how Majid, the seventh brother, found himself all alone, in front of his computer.

He didn't even know the screen inside the box was called a monitor. The New Generation BIT computers came in a wide range of colours, and this one was a handsome electric blue. A small BIT logo was stamped on the keyboard, across a picture of the globe.

Mrs Badach spread a lace tablecloth over the dining table. "Now to put it," she said in hushed tones. Computers made you clever. If Haziz had been into computers, he wouldn't have done all those stupid things. "Where iz rimote control?" Emmay wanted to know.

"It doesn't work like that," her son said dryly. His mum obviously didn't know the first thing about computers. In fact, Majid had a sneaking suspicion his mum didn't know much about anything at all.

He took the keyboard out of the box, along with the mouse, the speakers, the cables and the hard drive: each part made him even more confused. There was an enormous manual to go with the computer. He flicked through it until he came to the section written in English – "the common code" as Mr Mullins would have called it. Unfortunately the manual's authors hadn't written it with a twelve-year-old "receiver" in mind. It was like trying to understand the gobbledegook in 8D's English textbook.

"Aargh!" He heaved a sigh, throwing the manual down.

"Where iz button to learn Inglish?" Mrs Badach asked timidly.

"I don't know," he cried despairingly.

"Read the book, iz wrote in book."

"Oh, so you know how to read now, do you?" shouted Majid.

It was the first time he'd spoken to his mum like that.

"I never go to skool, my son," Mrs Badach replied with dignity. And she went into the kitchen.

Just then the doorbell rang. Maybe the delivery men had come back to set up the computer, like they'd done with the washing machine.

"Samir!" Majid nearly slammed the door in his classmate's face.

"Sorted?" said Samir. "Got your computer?"

He lived on the first floor of Hummingbird Tower, and he was green with envy.

Majid let him in as his only hope.

"Have you got one? I don't know how to set it up."

Samir pretended he knew what he was doing as he rattled the keyboard, picked up the mouse, examined the speakers, flicked through the manual.

"Right," he said, "right."

Majid felt more hopeful. "Well?"

"Just stick a few fish transfers on the screen, and you've got an aquarium."

News of Majid's technical hitch travelled fast on the estate. The next day, instead of saying hello, his friends asked, "How's your computer?"

Mrs Badach had put it back in its box, though not without a pang of regret.

In class, Hugh made the mistake of asking Majid, "How's the computer?"

Which set 8D off.

"Sir, the mouse got ate by Majid's cat."

"Sir, Majid's mum put the aerial on top and tried to pick up Couscous TV."

Majid leapt out of his chair and threw himself at Mamadou. "You *dare* talk about my mum!"

Hugh stood up just as quickly. "Majid, get back to your seat!"

"Fight!" brayed Samir.

"Samir, get out," ordered Hugh, not holding out much hope. "Majid, come and see me at the end of the lesson. Mamadou, I want to check your report sheet."

Samir didn't budge and Mamadou said he'd lost his report sheet ages ago.

When the bell rang, Majid tried to sneak out.

"Majid!" called Hugh.

"What?"

When 8D thought they were being blamed for something, they jerked their necks forward as if they were going to head-butt you. Just like Majid was doing now.

"It sounds like you're having a few problems installing your computer."

Majid frowned and looked even meaner.

"I'm not making fun of you."

Majid relaxed. "I don't know about computers."

"And your dad couldn't..."

Majid looked out of the window.

"What if I was to help you?" It was the first

time Hugh had ventured into the private life of one of his students.

"D'you mean it, sir?"

"Well, I know a bit about IT."

Hugh was single, and he spent every evening surfing the Net.

"Emmay, it's my teacher!" Majid called out, tossing his schoolbag across the living room.

Mrs Badach came out of her kitchen smiling and overwhelmed. She'd never been to school, but school was now coming to her.

"Mr Teacher," she corrected her son. "Spik Inglish proper. Hello, Mr Teacher, how you iz doing?"

Hugh hesitated. Should he shake hands or give her a peck on the cheek? He stood there awkwardly. "Fine, thank you, Mrs Badach. What about this computer, then?"

But he wasn't getting off that lightly. The cakes had been baked. Mrs Badach poured the mint tea in one continuous flow, slowly raising the teapot spout above the little coloured glasses, without spilling a single drop.

"Majid, he do work, innit?" she asked, sitting opposite the teacher. "I tell to him, work, work!"

"He could try a little harder," said Hugh with considerable tact. Majid never made a blind bit of effort.

"You hear, Majid? To try a littel harder!" She wanted to sound strict, but tears welled up in her eyes as soon as she looked at her son.

To divert his teacher's attention Majid tapped the screen, which hadn't been switched on yet.

"That's an impressive machine," said Hugh. "I've never seen a monitor this colour before. And a New Generation BIT is state of the art."

"Komputer iz good for skool?" Mrs Badach asked hopefully.

Hugh knew Majid would only use it for slaughtering the enemy, chainsawing limbs and splattering blood and brains. In other words, for having fun.

"He'll need the Internet," he said.

"Yes? Iz more good?"

"She hasn't got a clue," Majid muttered. He felt ashamed. Ashamed of the drab light in the living room, of the lace tablecloth under the computer, of his mother not knowing anything. And at the same time he was proud enough to be ashamed of being ashamed.

Majid needed the Internet. The Internet would change his life. But he didn't realize how much…

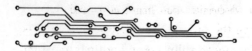

Magic Berber

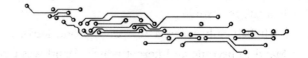

Hugh was reading 8D's book reports. They made him laugh out loud one moment and feel depressed the next.

"Ah, Nouria," he murmured. "Right ... where's Aisha's?"

Aisha and Nouria always handed in the same homework, apparently without realizing they were cheating. It meant one less piece of marking for Hugh.

The two girls had chosen Agatha Christie's *Murder on the Orient Express*. They'd written: *Its a who-dunnit. I really liked it. I didnt understood why they done it and the beginnings to long. Another thing, the characters isnt nice* and I dont like whodunnits. Apart from that its good.

Hugh gave the girls a 2, so they scraped a pass, and gazed longingly at his computer. Its screen was lit up day and night. It was his other life, his other world. Ping! Majid's logged on, thought Hugh, and it made him smile.

It had only taken a few one-to-one lessons for Majid to become an Internet whizz. Majid was terrible at English and his book report would probably be atrocious. But when it came to computers, he'd understood in a matter of weeks what other people took months to get to grips with. Hugh had given him his IP address: 194.129.64.221.

Whenever Majid went online, he always started by sending his teacher a message. But Hugh didn't want to be distracted today. There was still a big pile of reports to mark. He looked for Majid's.

Majid had chosen *Groosham Grange* by Anthony Horowitz, and he'd copied the fourth paragraph straight off the back cover: *When David Eliot is expelled from school, he's sent to a strange educational establishment on sinister Skrull Island. A novel shot through with dark humour. For eleven and up.*

You forgot the bar code, Hugh wrote at the top of

the page. Then, hesitating before he gave Majid the unsatisfactory 1 he deserved, he looked up. The screen was glowing in the half-light of his study.

Without thinking, Hugh wandered over to the computer. Sure enough, there was a message from Majid, who'd chosen Magic Berber as his user name on Internet Relay Chat. The screen flashed up:

> <Magic_Berber> hi! u ok? no work this eevning. wanna play?

Typing hadn't improved Majid's spelling. Hugh resisted the urge to reply. He didn't have time to play. He had work to do.

Another message appeared:

> <Magic_Berber> hey you there? i know u r there anser me. you plonker.

Hugh winced. He remembered his colleagues' advice: don't get too friendly with your students. He'd told Majid not to call him by his first name or chat informally on screen. So Majid called him by his player's name, Calimero, which wasn't much better.

<Magic_Berber> yo calimero wanna game
of counter-strike?

Hugh stifled a laugh and sat down, straddling his swivel chair in front of the computer. Counter-Strike was the crustiest, most retro-gory game you could play. And Hugh was an expert. Unable to contain himself any longer, he typed:

<Calimero> I've just got back from school
and read your message. Are you sure
you've finished all your homework?

He pressed ENTER and waited for an answer, his head flopped on his arms.

<Magic_Berber> liar! u woz there. u ready
4 a punchup?

Hugh laughed. Eyes shining with excitement, he replied:

<Calimero> Watch out, you asked for it!
But not more than fifteen minutes.

An hour later, Hugh was still attacking the evil terrorists, his ears on fire, his brain pulp.

"*Dooff-dooff!*" He imitated the sound effects of bombs exploding. "They've got me now!" he yelled with every defeat.

"You're all alone?" came a surprised voice from behind him.

"Hmm? Yes … almost." Hugh was embarrassed – his mum had caught him red-handed being a big kid.

"I'm going to Big B Stores," Mrs Mullins went on, sounding reproachful.

"OK," her son answered automatically. "You bumhead!"

"I beg your pardon?"

"No, not you. D'you want me to go shopping for you? Hey, take that! *Dooff-dooff!*"

"I wouldn't want to interrupt you," retorted Mrs Mullins sarcastically.

Hugh sighed when he heard the door shut. His mum had distracted him. He was going to lose.

Just as he was staging a comeback, his screen went red all over.

Blood red.

"What now?" Hugh was about to lose his temper.

A burst of violin music drowned out the sub-machine guns. Black letters slithered down the screen and vanished. Hugh was too busy frantically yanking his mouse to pay any attention. The next minute, everything had disappeared and the computer had gone off-line. Had Majid made a mistake, or had something gone wrong with the server?

"This is *ridiculous!*"

Hugh had now officially lost his temper.

There was nothing for it but to get back to his marking.

Majid had English next morning. Classes with Mr Mullins felt like a different kind of torture now. Majid was scared of giving himself away with a gesture or a look. It was all getting out of hand: the girls' feistiness, Mamadou's rowdiness and Samir's comments. As the minutes went by, seeing poor Calimero's face falling made him want to shout, "Leave him alone, can't you?"

He was hoping for a quiet word with Hugh, because something weird had happened to his computer, as well as his mum's electric kettle. But if he was seen talking to the teacher, he'd be branded a geek. And Sebastian was the only one who got called that.

"Morning, sir!" said Majid as he walked into the classroom.

Magic Berber and Calimero clicked at first glance. Hugh raised his eyebrows, which meant "What happened last night?" Majid put 8D's register on the desk and whispered, "Is yours working again?"

"Yes," murmured Hugh, before quickly shouting, "Samir, find somewhere to sit that's not *on* Farida!"

"It's OK, sir. She likes it."

Hugh closed his eyes. He already felt tired. He was in for another hour in the bullring, where the kids shouted "RA-AA-AH!" instead of "Olé!" for every hit. "Take out a clean sheet of paper," he said wearily. "We're going to do a dictation."

"Oh no, sir, *please!*" begged Nouria and Aisha, holding hands.

"I always get trashed in your dictations, man," Mamadou bellowed. "There's no point writing anything. You just fail me straight off."

"That's enough, Mamadou!" said Hugh, losing

his temper. Again. "Give me your report sheet."

"Like I told you, I lost it," answered the tall kid from Senegal. "LOST IT! You get me?"

Hugh was hitting rock bottom.

"Are we doing this dictation or what?" asked Majid, offering some back-up.

Calimero gave him a friendly glance, but the next second Majid got hit on the head. It was Zeinul, who was sitting behind him.

"So you like dictations, hey, geek?"

It had happened. Majid's worst nightmare. Being lumped with Sebastian, the only good student in 8D.

But Hugh was getting the hang of his class. If he told Zeinul off for hitting Majid, 8D would shout "Poor little Majid!" So he carried straight on with the dictation.

"'A Walk in the Snow...' That's the title. Turn round, Majid. You can sort things out with Zeinul at break."

"Is there a full stop after 'break'?" asked Samir, who was writing *You can sort things out with Zeinul...*

"I wasn't dictating then, Samir," said Hugh, sounding increasingly detached. "But I am now. 'As

a child comma I understood the explorer's joy—'
Mamadou, try not to be so obvious when you're
cheating. 'The explorer's joy when he enters—'"

"Not so fast! Not so fast!" moaned Nouria and
Aisha.

"What comes after 'explorer'?" murmured
Miguel, to nobody in particular.

"Joy!" bellowed Mamadou from the back of the
classroom.

"'The explorer's joy'," said Hugh as if the lesson
was going perfectly to plan, "'joy when he enters
virgin territory…'"

"Yeah, Farida, they're talking about you!" said
Samir.

And 8D creased up. For five minutes, nobody
wrote a single word.

That evening, Hugh took the dictations out of his
bag. He looked for Sebastian's straight away and
gave him a 5 for excellent. Then he got ready to
line up the 1s. Magic Berber had a surprise for him:

*Yestirday I saw somefing on my screen when we woz
playing. It woz a blud red picture with black leters like*

the name of a game. I think the name woz a word like Gogol but i didn't read it proper. The worst thing woz a kind of scary violyn music. I woz scared and I called my mum. But she woz scared to coz her electrik ketel sparked and cort fire. Thats it.

Hugh had to read it through twice more to make sense of what Majid had written. Then, at the top of the page, he wrote: If this is your dictation, your mark is 0. If it's an essay, I'm impressed by your imagination! And because he was just a big kid at heart, he gave Majid a 3 for well tried.

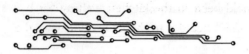

Something in the Wires?

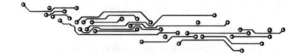

Majid's mum was cross. Her electric kettle had stopped working. It was very odd.

The evening before, Majid had been playing on his computer in the living room. Mrs Badach had heard triumphant whoops followed by angry swearing, but she hadn't batted an eyelid. As far as she was concerned, it must be proper English if Majid was playing with his teacher. Mrs Badach imagined a long cable buried underneath the tarmac, linking her son's computer to Mr Mullins's. She worried about cutting off the electricity supply in Mr Teacher's house every time she turned out the lights.

While she'd been in the kitchen waiting for her tea to cool, she'd heard a frightened shout from the living room.

"Emmay!"

Just then the kettle had sparked and the kitchen had filled with the smell of burning plastic.

"Majid!"

They'd rushed towards each other.

"What iz matter?"

Majid had explained to his mum what he'd seen on his screen. Then he'd had a close look at the kettle.

"It's brucked, innit?"

Mrs Badach was particularly cross because the kettle was a brand-new present from Mr Badach. She went back to Big B Stores, where he'd bought it, and approached a sales assistant in a red jacket who was busy doing nothing.

"Hello, mister, how you iz doing?" she asked politely.

"Whaddya want, Fatima?"

"Iz for kettle, mister. My huzband he just buyed it and iz brucked, innit?"

The sales assistant's eyes bulged. He took the kettle from Mrs Badach, saw the melted plastic and said patronizingly, "Listen, Fatima, you don't put electric goods on the stove. D'you understand?"

Mrs Badach understood perfectly. The sales assistant was a racist and he took her for an idiot.

"Thank you, mister," she said with calm dignity. "But I iz not so stupid like you think. And my name it iz not Fatima."

When Mrs Badach got back to Hummingbird Tower with her broken kettle, the lift was out of order. For a moment, she felt somebody had it in for her. But then Majid caught up with her on his way back from school. He looked so grown up with his bag slung over one shoulder, Emmay's heart melted faster than her kettle. She wanted to say to her son: "Your eyes shine like stars, and my thoughts are always with you, when you're asleep, when you go out, when you come home." But she just put his jacket collar up and asked, "You waz not cold this morning?"

"Aargh, man! The lift's brucked!" moaned Majid, taking no notice of her. He was about to start climbing the stairs with his mum, when he heard a slight noise. He turned round. Aisha was behind him.

"It's out of order," he said, because he didn't know what else to say.

"Well, I guess the exercise keeps you fit," replied the girl from Mali, who didn't know what to say either.

"It's like a workout." Majid was struggling.

They both burst out laughing. They'd been eyeing each other for a few weeks now. Majid wouldn't admit to liking Aisha, but he'd have given his right arm to wind her up the way Samir did Farida.

"Oh no!"

They both said it at the same time. The light in the stairwell had just gone out.

"Majid, give me your hand!" Emmay shrieked.

"Give us a break," her son grumbled.

In the dark he caught hold of Aisha's hand instead, and they walked up the last three flights together. The landing light was working and Aisha immediately let go. She'd been brought up very strictly. She was feisty at school, but silent at home.

"Bye!" she said.

"We've got loads of homework tonight," called Majid, kicking himself because he couldn't think of anything funny to say.

Emmay was looking for the keys in her shopping bag. Majid watched Aisha disappear into her flat, just across from his.

In the living room, one glance at his computer cheered Majid up.

> <Calimero> I've been warming up a load of aliens for you. Ready when you are for Special Warrior.

This was one of their favourite games, "not recommended for players under sixteen". Majid threw his bag, jacket and scarf on the floor. Forgetting he had loads of homework to do, he typed feverishly:

> <Magic_Berber> send them over i'm gonna kill the hole lot. You wont no wots hit you.

Hugh cringed but sent the game over the network all the same. He'd spent his last free morning on the rocket launcher. It was a lethal weapon. Now he wanted to show off to an expert who'd appreciate his skills. He was in a trance when, twenty minutes later, his screen suddenly turned red.

"Not again!" he fumed. "I don't believe it!"

But this time, instead of messing about with the mouse, he kept his eyes glued to the monitor. Black letters slithered down it. A word appeared. Just one.

Golem

"Golem," whispered Hugh.

And a deep voice answered *"Golemmmm"*, stressing the o and making the m hum. A figure appeared on the left of the screen, a tiny gleaming warrior in helmet and boots. He was spinning a spiky golden ball on the end of a chain. Back view, front view, back view, front view, the warrior spun round like a hammer thrower, getting bigger and bigger towards the middle of the screen. Close up, the helmet hid his face completely.

The warrior turned his back on Hugh and froze with his feet wide apart, as if waiting for a battle signal. The violins that had screeched to a crescendo while he was spinning suddenly hushed. Then came a rattling sound like an old typewriter. Words appeared on the screen one letter at a time, but in rapid succession.

Enter your name.

There was a medieval-looking scroll below this command.

It was a game, Hugh realized. A pirate game that had just hijacked the one Magic Berber and Calimero had been playing. He typed **Calimero** and his player's name appeared on the scroll, white on black. Still with his back turned, the warrior swung the ball above his head. Then he froze again, awating further instructions. But who from?

Hugh hesitated. How were you meant to play this game? Presumably by clicking on the mouse and pressing a few keys. He might as well have a go at moving the little warrior around. He put his hand on the mouse and right-clicked. The warrior brandished the chain in his right arm. Hugh left-clicked and the warrior lifted his left arm.

Calimero smiled. "You're nervous, boyo."

He slid the mouse forward. The warrior disappeared from view. A pile of weapons at the bottom of the screen was the only indication that he was still there. It was as if Hugh had become the warrior controlling the weapons.

Basically, it was an old-fashioned shoot-out. Not really his kind of game. He preferred weapons that blew you up from a distance – dooff-dooff! – to bone-smashing bludgeons. As if the computer could read his thoughts, a flurry of letters splattered onto the screen.

Choose your weapon, Calimero!

"Weird."

Hugh liked the way the programmers called the player by the name he'd typed on the scroll. It made it more interactive.

"But how d'you choose your weapon?" he wondered aloud.

No chance to find out. Suddenly the image jumped, the screen turned red again and the computer went off-line.

He really wanted to phone Majid. Had he played this game? Had he even heard of it?

"Golem," Hugh repeated. He pulled a face. He read magazines like *Generation 4* and *Joystick*.

But he couldn't remember reading anything about a game called Golem. Maybe it was an old one. He made a mental note to visit the computer games section at Big B Stores. But for now, what mattered was finding out who kept interrupting them. A moronic hacker? A virus? A bug? Was someone deliberately targeting them? What a horrible thought. And if so, how could he track them down?

When he turned the light out to go to sleep, he could still see the little helmeted warrior in the left-hand corner of his brain. Turning, turning, turning, back, front, back. That spiky ball didn't seem so scary when you thought about everything else out there: monsters, hardened criminals, the students of 8D. He vowed to track down Golem.

The next day was Saturday. Hugh didn't have to go to work. He offered to do the shopping for his mum.

"If you like," said Mrs Mullins, pleasantly surprised. "And why don't you get your hair cut while you're at it? I can't see your eyes."

Gently she brushed a few strands of hair off his

face. Hugh didn't react, because he was thinking of something else. Thinking of…

"Golem?" repeated the girl in Big B Stores.

"It's the name of a game," said Hugh shyly.

The girl smiled. He was cute, she decided. Skinny, wide-eyed, a bit lost, but definitely cute.

"Are you sure about the name? Because there's nothing like that here."

"I saw it on the Net. Maybe … maybe it's not in the shops yet," he stammered. "It … it doesn't matter."

The girl kept on smiling and staring at him. Hugh had a hunch that if he said "Are you free this evening?" the answer would probably be yes.

Time to go.

"Doesn't matter," he said again. "Thank you."

He felt mildly depressed by the time he got back home. He was twenty-six and his only girlfriends were an Australian from Canberra and a Canadian from Toronto. He'd never met either of them and never expected to. He had virtual love affairs and his best friend was twelve years old. There had to be a serious bug in his personal program.

"I didn't go to the barber's," he told his mother aggressively as he dumped the shopping in the kitchen.

Mrs Mullins was distracted. "The microwave's stopped working. It gave me a scare. It sparked when I tried to use it."

Hugh had a feeling he'd recently heard a similar story. Who'd mentioned something to him about short-circuiting and sparks?

The Little Warrior

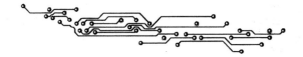

Even a Mega B pizza leaflet through Mrs Badach's letter box was an event. So a letter, a *real* letter, called for a celebration.

"You read it me?" Mrs Badach asked, sitting cross-legged as if she was meditating.

"It's from Price Shrinkers again," explained Majid. "OK, here we go: 'Dear sir...' Get that, they think I'm a grown-up! 'Dear sir, we hope you are entirely satisfied with the New Generation BIT computer that you won in our last competition. We'd like to photograph you in front of your computer for our spring/summer catalogue. As a goodwill gesture for any inconvenience caused, we are pleased to offer you a PC game of your choice from pages 237–8.' Wicked!"

He looked up and saw panic in his mum's eyes.

"But my hair, iz so big mess," she cried.

"That doesn't matter. It's me they want a picture of."

"But wallpaper iz trashed. And for stain on ceiling? Iz not possible, Majid. What they will be thinking, Price Shrinkers?"

Majid looked up at the ceiling and saw an enormous damp patch. He groaned. "Why are we poor?"

"Nobody he iz poor, my son, if he got dignity," Emmay answered.

A hair appointment was duly made. Mr Badach repainted the ceiling and put up new wallpaper. Everything was ready for the Price Shrinkers.

The following Tuesday, a photographer and his assistant turned up at the Badachs'. The photographer seemed very enthusiastic about his shoot.

"T'rrific!" he exclaimed, spinning round to get a better view of the tiny living-room-diner. "Loads of atmosphere. Know what I mean, Marco?"

"And look at wallpaper?" asked Mrs Badach proudly.

"Ace! Check it out, Marco. Babar the Elephant wallpaper, nice vibe!" He turned to his assistant, who was looking fazed. "We'll take the lady's portrait. With the kid, and the lace tablecloth under the blue computer, the works, know what I mean? T'rrific! Hey, Marco, how about we stick the reflector over there? And the spotlight here!"

It was like watching a bad comedy sketch. Majid sat down in front of his computer and read the message that had just flashed up.

<Calimero> Who are we killing today?

Majid gave the photographer a dirty look and muttered, "Dooff-dooff!" But he'd have to take it out on the aliens instead.

Five minutes later he was interrupted for the third time by the game Hugh and Majid hadn't been able to find for sale anywhere. Just as before, the screen turned red, the letters **Golem** were displayed and the little warrior appeared.

"Absolutely fabulous!" the photographer gushed behind him. "OK, if the kid can shift a bit to the right so we can see the screen. And the lady needs to move in closer. That's it. Smashing! Not your average fashion shoot, know what I'm saying?"

He took twenty photos of mother and son together. "T'rrific! Ace! Fab! It's a wrap. You're on your way to celebrity. Hollywood and all that... Be seeing ya, kid!" He breezed out.

Majid shrugged. The screen had just displayed the words:

Choose your weapon, <u>M</u>agic Berber!

Majid desperately hoped the little warrior wouldn't disappear again like he had before.

"Stay there," he whispered.

There were no instructions. He'd have to work the game out by trial and error. To choose your weapon in Special Warrior, you had to press the] key. Majid chanced it.

The screen answered:

Try harder, <u>M</u>agic Berber!

The M was underlined again. Instinctively Majid pressed that key. Four weapons appeared in the right-hand corner of the screen in dull shades of grey: an axe, a javelin, a sling and a bow. Suddenly Majid felt as let down by the game as he did by his life.

"Aargh, man!"

All the same, he clicked on the bow, which detached itself from the others and spun in mid-air. The 3D effect was impressive. The warrior held out his arm and the bow fitted neatly into it. He let out a short, triumphant "Yee-ha!"

"So…?" Magic Berber muttered. The warrior was never going to wipe out psychopaths or aliens or terrorists with tiny arrows like that.

Still guessing, Majid pressed the up arrow on the keyboard. The little warrior turned and sent an arrow flying up the screen. A hollow *schtok!* made the computer vibrate. The arrow had landed in something. But what?

Majid started playing around with the four arrows on the keyboard – up, down, left, right. The warrior fired with breathtaking speed. His arrows went whistling through the air before landing in invisible targets.

"Nang!" he exclaimed. Suddenly he wanted to conquer the world with a bow in his hand. He'd kill the enemy, find the treasure and marry Princess Aisha. Majid had played a lot of different games. But he'd never felt the urge to fight like this before. The Force was with him.

"Get a move on," he said to the little warrior.

In Special Warrior you had to press the Q key to move forward. But in this game Q made the tiny man leap dangerously. Laughing, he pressed the space bar instead. The warrior set off, *toc, toc*. Majid turned round. The echoing footsteps were so realistic they filled the living room.

He spent the next ten minutes testing different command options. It was up to him to work out the rules. C made the little warrior crawl, and when you pressed 1 the arrow caught fire. But he still needed to find out how to start the game. In Special Warrior you pressed ESC and a menu popped up offering varying levels of difficulty. But so far, Golem just seemed to be about the little warrior's physical training. Majid could feel his frustration growing. What was the point? So what if the warrior was armed and ready to fight, when nobody else knew about it?

Suddenly the rattling started again.

To find out what your first mission is, type E.

Then the screen went blurry and the game disappeared.

"Not again!" Majid shouted.

He was frustrated. Angry. Heartbroken. He had to have this game. He had to have this game. He *had* to have this game!

The next day in English, Majid realized that Hugh was in a state too. But they had to wait for the end of class to talk about it. Majid dropped his pencil case so he could stay behind.

Hugh came over. He didn't really know what to say. *Don't get too friendly with your students.* He could feel his colleagues watching him.

"Any problems last night?" he asked casually.

"How far did you get?" said Majid eagerly. "I couldn't carry out my first mission."

"Nor could I! But I got my weapon."

"The bow? Nice one!"

"I got a flame-thrower."

"Dooff-dooff?"

"No, it goes *whoosh*. But it's lethal. It wipes out everything within a hundred-metre range."

They looked at each other, confused. The game seemed to hijack whatever program they were already playing.

"To make him move forward—" Majid began.

"—you press the space bar. And have you seen how he kicks when you press ALT?"

"And Q? That's a killer leap."

"I started writing it all down. Otherwise we'll forget."

Silence.

"It's kind of weird, though," said Majid hesitantly.

"Maybe it's an advertisement," mused Hugh. "For the launch of a new game."

"You have to see me shooting my flaming arrows! *Zzzzippp!*" Majid mimed them whizzing through the air. "They'd rip you to shreds. And the flames look totally real."

"Wait till there's bleeding. It's going to look better than the real thing!"

Hugh heard a noise and turned round. Samir was at the classroom door, listening.

Samir looked like he was going for one of 8D's famous head-butts. He wanted to lash out. But he was too shocked to say anything. Majid and a teacher talking like old friends? He turned on his heels. For the first time in his life, he was clean out of words.

He headed back to Hummingbird Tower, deep in thought. There were two Samirs. One was feisty and loud, a crowd-pleaser. The other was tragically lonely.

"Dear Majid, *nice* Majid," he kept saying between gritted teeth. Majid with his dad who worked day and night. Samir's dad was unemployed. Majid with his six brothers. Samir had one little sister. A little sister who was very sick. Majid with Emmay, and her delicious cakes and mint tea. Samir's mum smoked in bed until midday.

And now Majid was betraying 8D. Going over to the teacher's side. He'd pay for it.

Samir would never admit it, but he'd have given anything to be in Majid's shoes. Stupid Majid. Loser Majid. Majid the geek. Samir felt like he was going to explode with anger. Anger. And pain.

He worked out what to do as he walked along. He'd start hanging out with Majid. Yes, that was it. And then he'd get him into trouble and bring shame to the Badach family for generations to come. Yes, that was what he'd do. He'd prove to that nobody English teacher that Majid was worth the same as Samir.

Nothing.

Aisha Doesn't Want People Talking About Her

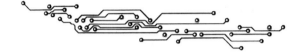

Majid was the youngest. Aisha was the eldest. It made a world of difference.

Aisha had three brothers and a baby sister. She started work the moment she got home. And that didn't mean maths homework. She went to buy the bread, she took the washing out of the machine, she kept an eye on her little brother who was learning to walk, and she gave her baby sister her bottle. Then she laid the table, dropped the noodles into boiling water and changed her sister's nappy.

"Aisha! Aisha!"

Her mum kept calling her until bedtime. There was always something to do. Her mum wasn't an unreasonable woman. She was just run off her feet. And her dad was strict. He lashed out at the slightest provocation. A slap for the little brother who broke a glass. One for the baby, who cried during the news. One for Aisha for not stopping her brother from breaking the glass, and another for watching TV instead of keeping the baby quiet. It wasn't a living hell. But it wasn't a life either.

One day, Aisha had said to Nouria, "I'm a robot at home." Sometimes, in her head, she pretended to be a robot and said in a mechanical voice, "Change the baby: baby changed. Gut the fish: fish gutted…"

In bed she dreamt she lived on a different planet. She was Princess Aisha, and she got to order all the robots about. She told them to write her book report, because Mr Mullins was nice but she didn't have time to do her homework. Luckily she copied everything off Nouria.

But on Thursday she was out of luck. Nouria was away, and they had a test.

"Hey, Majid," Aisha said in the corridor, "can I sit next to you in English?"

Majid didn't kid himself. It wasn't that she liked him. It was because they had a test. "You'd get a better mark sitting next to Sebastian."

"Yuck! He's a geek!"

Aisha didn't even want a good mark. Just a pass, so she wouldn't get blasted at home. She sat down next to Majid, right in front of the teacher. Hugh had already written the instructions on the board: *Choose an adjective, for example "interesting" or "amusing", and make up a sentence to give its comparative ("more") and superlative ("most") forms.*

They were starting to whisper at the back of the class. Mamadou was blatantly looking up the answers.

"Mamadou, put your dictionary away or I'll fail you straight off!"

"Just checking, sir," bellowed Mamadou indignantly.

For a few minutes, 8D were almost hard-working.

"Majid," said Hugh, "why don't you just hand your test to Aisha? That way she won't get a stiff neck."

People started sniggering because he had linked Majid and Aisha.

"Go for it, Majid!" shouted Miguel.

Magic Berber gave Calimero an exasperated look, as if to say, "Aargh, man! Now you've *really* landed me in it." Samir spotted the glance. This friendship made him see red.

Hugh moved between the rows, living dangerously among the troublemakers. On his way past, he glanced at what Majid had written: *Golem is a safe game, Calimero is a bare safe gamer, but Magic Berber is nang!* Hugh couldn't help sighing.

"What?" said Majid sharply, looking up.

Calimero put a hand on his shoulder to reassure him, and went back to his desk. The advantage of having a test was that 8D were quiet.

Suddenly Hugh caught Samir's eye. "Have you finished, Samir?"

"No," the boy said, deliberately slowly. "I've only just begun."

And he didn't make any of his usual rowdy comments for the rest of the lesson.

At the end of the afternoon, Majid sidled up to Aisha. "D'you want to walk home together?"

After Mr Mullins's remark in class, Aisha knew

it would look bad if she walked back with Majid. "I've got to pick up my brother," she mumbled, to get rid of him.

Majid looked away, as if he'd never wanted to speak to her in the first place. So they walked home separately, each taking a different route, Aisha thinking of Majid and Majid thinking of Aisha. That was how it was.

"Aisha!" her mum shouted as soon as she came in through the door. "I've run out of baby milk!"

Aisha put her bag down and stared at the wall in front of her. Tired. She was tired. It was dark. A cold February night.

"Aisha!" screamed her mum. "D'you hear me? Or your father'll have something to say!"

Tears welled up in Aisha's eyes. "All right, I'm going," she shouted back.

She took her mum's purse from the kitchen and went out, slamming the door. She pressed the lift button and waited. For a long time. She pressed it once more.

"Not again," she moaned, kicking the door.

The lift was out of order. She walked down the stairs, three at a time, and at every floor her heart felt lighter. She wasn't the kind of person to bear a grudge.

Big B Stores was on the other side of the Moreland Estate. Aisha didn't like it. A crew of older boys always hung out there, leaning on their mopeds. They made comments about her because she was pretty, with her long neck and almond-shaped eyes.

When she reached the supermarket, there they were in spite of the cold. Two of the leaders revved their engines. Another had brought his stereo and was blaring out Khaled's latest CD. Aisha wished she could slip past, as invisible as a grey cat in the dark.

"Aisha!" shouted a voice she recognized.

It was Samir. He came striding over to her. "Well, I never. On the Koran of Mecca! You seeing Majid?"

"Listen," said the slip of a girl, "I don't talk about you, so don't talk about me."

She spoke with such vehemence that Samir took a step backwards. "I-ain't-talk-ing-'bout-ya-Ai-sha," he rapped, hopping from foot to foot, ready to dodge if she tried to hit him. "Coz-I-don't-like-ya.

But we know somebody who does, you get me? Majid likes you, Aisha!"

Aisha raised an arm. Samir dodged, shouting out at the top of his voice, "I'm not talking *about* you, Aisha, I'm talking *for* Majid! He's shy!"

"Fool," Aisha muttered under her breath.

She was angry and happy at the same time. Had Majid told Samir he'd held her hand on the stairs? It wasn't the kind of thing you mentioned. Otherwise people would be talking about her. Laughing behind her back. "Majid and Aisha, phwoar!" But what if Majid really did like her?

When she got back to Hummingbird Tower, there was a nasty surprise waiting for her. As if the lift being out of order wasn't enough, the timer-switch for the light in the stairwell had stopped working too. Climbing up twelve flights of stairs on your own in the dark was bad enough. But bumping into somebody was worse.

Aisha held onto the icy handrail and felt for the first step with her foot. She still couldn't see anything by the time she reached the first floor, but she was getting used to climbing blind. She tried not to breathe too hard, so nobody would notice her. But the noise still seemed to fill the stairwell. She was counting in her head. Fourth. Fifth.

Suddenly she heard a door opening on the next landing. Somebody pressed the light switch, realized it wasn't working, and swore loudly. It was a man.

All kinds of schoolgirl horror stories were going round in Aisha's head. Meetings on the stairs. Basement attacks. Rumours. *You know that red-haired girl nobody ever saw again...* Terrified, she flattened herself against the wall. She heard heavy footsteps and panting. He must be a big man. He wasn't going very fast. He stopped to curse. Then off he went again. He was so close when he passed her. Too close... Aisha could smell his cigarette. She pressed her body so hard against the wall it hurt. *Ouch.* The man carried on down the stairs. Thank you, God. Not caring whether anybody could hear her or not, she ran the rest of the way up to the twelfth floor.

She was so relieved to reach her own landing, she burst out laughing and buried her face in her hands. Wait till she told Nouria about this. She'd exaggerate a bit. Say the man had brushed against her.

When she'd finally calmed down, Aisha looked up. Her jaw dropped.

Despite the dark, she could see a thin trail of smoke rising up to the ceiling. Where was it coming from? Not from her flat. Phew. From the other side of the corridor.

"Majid," she whispered.

The smoke looked like it was coming from under his door.

"Fire!" she said in a choked voice.

But the smoke didn't smell of fire. And it was blue. A bluish white, lit up from inside. It spread out the higher it got, undulating with the slightest current of air. Every so often, flashes of light sparked across it and an electric blue charge crackled around the edge. What was going on at the Badachs'?

Aisha didn't dare get any closer. She just wanted to be back with the little ones and her mum calling "Aisha! Aisha!" Hugging the wall, she made her way over to her flat, still staring at the smoke. She took the key out of her pocket and opened the door.

"Aisha, you took your time! Your father's back."

The young girl looked behind her. The corridor was in darkness. The smoke had vanished. She closed the door with her heel and stood there for a few seconds, petrified.

"What's the matter?" her dad asked roughly. "Are you ill?"

Aisha put her hand to her forehead. Was she going mad? "No, I'm OK," she stammered. "I've been running."

She wasn't used to confiding in people. Not even her best friend.

The next day at break, Aisha caught sight of Majid and decided to keep an eye on him. The smoke had been coming from his place. He must have noticed.

"All right?" she asked him.

"Yeah. Samir said he saw you last night."

Aisha bristled. "What d'you mean, he said he saw me?"

Majid took a step back. "You know, outside Big B Stores."

Aisha shrugged. News travelled fast on the Moreland Estate. "Boys gossip just as much as girls," she said scornfully. "There's nothing wrong with going to Big B Stores."

"Who said there was?"

Failed again. Majid was trying to impress Aisha with the fact that he was hanging out with Samir. But it hadn't worked.

"Get this: don't *ever* talk to Samir about me again," she hissed.

Majid felt a big lump in his throat. He didn't like her anyway. Or maybe, just a bit.

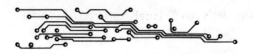

Golemia

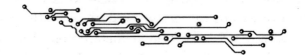

Every so often, suspicious games appear on the Internet and then disappear again, without anybody knowing how or why. Hugh couldn't see where Golem's programmers wanted to take their players. What kind of universe was he entering? What was he looking for?

One evening, after typing the letter E, he found himself staring at his first mission. The screen opened from the middle, like theatre curtains, and stunning graphics appeared. There was a corridor with flares casting an eerie glow on old portraits. Somewhat predictably, there were three closed doors.

"OK, boyo, let's go," Hugh ordered the little warrior.

He pressed the space bar to move the warrior forward, and released it in front of the second door. How'd you get in? Hugh had the not al-together original idea of pressing ENTER. The door opened and he saw an enormous room that was dark and not very welcoming. It was too late to turn back now.

Toc, toc, toc, the warrior's footsteps rang out. A terrifying *grrmffussh!* came through the speakers. A dragon! Hugh quickly pressed 6 to recover his flame-thrower.

"You won't know what's hit you, monster!" he exclaimed.

The weapon spluttered a pathetic *whoosh.* The dragon retaliated with an enormous fiery breath.

"OK, forget it."

The warrior was a pile of ashes and the screen flashed:

Burnt!
➤ start play
➤ end play

Hugh clicked on **start play** without wasting any time. He was worried the game would suddenly uninstall itself again. He didn't have a clue how to access it.

"OK, this time we'll do it in order," Calimero reasoned out loud. "First door on the right."

The warrior entered a kind of throne room. But instead of a king on the purple cushion, there was … a leather muzzle. Hugh chuckled. An enormous muzzle for an enormous mouth.

"Duh … now *dat* would be for my dragon…"

He rushed the little warrior over to the muzzle, without paying any attention to the suits of armour on either side of the throne. They promptly sprang to life, each lowering a halberd. *Schlak schlak!* The suits of armour destroyed the little warrior.

"You idiot!" groaned Hugh.

Chopped up!
➢ start play
➢ end play

He started again, went back into the throne room, torched the suits of armour with his flame-thrower, *whoosh-whoosh*, and clicked on the muzzle. This time, he'd won. Well ... almost. With the muzzle in one hand, the little warrior went back into the second room and leapt to one side to avoid the dragon's fiery snorts. Hugh pressed the ALT key and the dragon got a giant kick in the nostrils.

Ow, ow, it groaned, collapsing on the ground.

The warrior put the muzzle on it.

"There you go," Calimero congratulated himself, "piece of cake!"

The programmers weren't so mean, after all. Hugh caught his breath. He admired the way the designers had done the scary shadows.

Technically and graphically, the game was to die for. The warrior walked realistically, and the dragon was hilarious. Its red eyes had turned blue. It was snoring at the warrior's feet, cute as a giant kitten. Flames were still coming out of its mouth, but they were just the splutterings of a baby dragon. The screen flashed:

To find out what your next mission is, type EM.

Hugh obeyed, and the dragon immediately raised its head. *Merrr merrr!* It gazed imploringly and started making whimpering sounds behind its muzzle. It wanted to say something, probably to tell Hugh which way to go. But how could he get the muzzle off? Instinctively he pressed ESC. Off it came. Those blue eyes turned red again. The dragon rose up on its hind legs and blew an enormous puff of fire. *Grrmffussh!* Onto the little warrior.

"No!" roared Hugh, sending his chair spinning backwards as if he was the one about to be burnt to a cinder.

The screen was gloating:

Ha ha, got you!

"What's going on?" asked Mrs Mullins, who'd come in because of all the noise.

"Huh? Nothing." Hugh tried to calm down. But he was on the brink of tears. "Nothing," he said again glumly.

Mrs Mullins gave him a long hard look and closed the door. She was a psychologist, and she sometimes wondered what she'd done to her son to stop him growing up.

With the determination of a veteran gamer, Hugh retraced his steps, but this time he didn't fall for the dragon's whimperings.

"Merrr merrr! to you too," he teased.

Unsure what to do, he moved the cursor around the screen, trying to figure how to get out. Suddenly, at the foot of one of the arches in the throne room, the arrow turned into a little hand inviting the player to click on it.

"What's that?" he muttered, narrowing his eyes. "It can't be...? Oh yes it is!"

It was a saddle. A saddle for riding the dragon. The little warrior climbed on and the screen opened up again.

"Wow!"

He was flying on the dragon's back. Below him was the castle he'd just been exploring. Beyond it lay hills and valleys, villages with smoking chimneys – a whole world. After a few moments of breathtaking flight, a map appeared in the left-hand corner of the screen. One of those old parchment maps where a cartographer has drawn caves, forests and mountains with more artistry than accuracy. The names of towns and rivers were handwritten in beautiful Gothic letters that were almost illegible.

At the same time, several objects popped up

at the bottom of the screen: a flask, a magnifying glass, a lamp, a compass and a key. Hugh clicked on the magnifying glass, which started moving all over the screen. He could read the names now: Tamza, Icaria, Tulamor and Golemia.

"Hmm ... Golemia," he said thoughtfully. "That must be the capital."

He moved the cursor over the map. The little arrow turned into a hand at every name. Could you get into these places with a simple click of the mouse? He tried his luck with Golemia. The dragon beat its wings, flew to the highest point in the sky, then dropped vertically towards a city encircled by walls. Golemia!

A new map appeared. It was a city plan.

"Amazing!" he whispered.

When he moved the magnifying glass, it showed the names of streets and alleys, squares, monuments and bridges: Crow Bridge, King Ivan V Street, Taliva Square, Hangers' Alley, Golden Goose Inn... The dragon flew over the city, a bustling, teeming place where you could easily imagine a market, a fortress, churches, slums and palaces.

Suddenly a shower of arrows crossed the screen.

Scary! There were archers on the city walls and they were firing at the dragon. An arrow pierced its wing.

"They're going to kill us, Bubble!"

In a moment of confusion, Hugh had given the dragon a name. Bubble started losing height. Using the mouse, Hugh turned him away from inhospitable Golemia. They landed in a field, between two haystacks. Hugh noticed a red bar emptying at the top of the screen. It was probably the dragon's life span or energy reserves. What should he do? Bubble was losing blood and whimpering. *Merrr merrr...*

Hugh had a flash of inspiration: the flask. One click and he grabbed it. The flask fitted neatly in the little warrior's hands as he gave the dragon his medicine. The red bar filled up. Saved! But the warrior wouldn't be able to use that flask again in this round.

Hugh was so engrossed in his dragon, in his warrior, in Golemia and its archers, that he didn't hear the phone.

"Hugh!" his mother called. She came into the study. "Hugh, it's for you!"

"Merrr merrr…" mumbled the young man, his eyes on the screen.

"For goodness' sake, Hugh. It's somebody from school. The science teacher."

Hugh looked at his mother as if she was talking in a foreign language, from another time or universe.

"The science teacher," Mrs Mullins said again, alarmed. "It's about the staff meeting."

"Yes," he said, trying to pull himself together. "The staff meeting, the science teacher." He wasn't quite there yet.

"Look!" his mother exclaimed.

The screen had gone red.

"No!" he shouted. "My game!"

Golem had uninstalled itself and Hugh hadn't even recorded his score.

"Oh no!" He was upset. Shattered. Heartbroken.

"Hugh, it's no good getting yourself all worked up like this…"

What Mrs Mullins wanted to say was: "I mean, come on, it's hardly real life. Get out, meet some girls, have some fun!" But she'd been scared of giving him hang-ups from the moment he was born. So she settled for: "Are you going to speak to her?"

Mrs Mullins had high hopes of the science teacher, who was a charming young woman in her opinion. She was called Nadia, she was blonde, she had a slight lisp and Hugh had mentioned her a few times in conversation. But, most importantly, Mrs Mullins had seen Nadia talking to her son after school one day. She was clearly in love with him. She laughed too loudly and she simpered. Any 8D watching would have called out, "Get in there, sir!"

But Hugh hadn't noticed anything. Except that the science teacher was blonde and had trouble pronouncing some of her words.

"Hello?" he said abruptly.

"Thugh? Am I interwupting you?"

"Not really," he replied, trying to sound friendly.

Nadia wanted to talk to him about the next staff meeting and the problem students in 8D. "I understand you're having some issues with Thamir?"

"No. I just want to kill him, that's all."

Nadia gave a little cough. This didn't seem to be one of her colleague's better days. "And we need to talk about the students who aren't diswuptive in class, but who don't make a blind bit of effort."

Hugh frowned. "Are you thinking of anybody in particular?"

"Mathid."

Aisha was also thinking about Majid in particular. She couldn't work out if they were annoyed with each other or not. They still said hello every morning. But he didn't ask "All right?" any more. The more she thought about it, the weirder she thought Majid was. What about that bluish smoke she'd seen coming out of his flat? She knew she hadn't imagined it.

One evening, on her way home from school, she plucked up the courage to walk over to the Badachs' door. The stairwell light had finally been mended, and she could see a long black mark on the wall, next to the door frame. Like a scorch mark. She held out her hand. As soon as she touched the wall, she got a slight shock. Nothing very painful. A bit like you sometimes get from a car door. Static electricity. But Aisha stepped back, frightened. The strange smoke had also crackled with sparks.

No, she definitely hadn't imagined it.

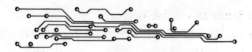

Golem City

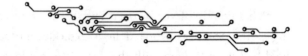

"He's no fool."

At least everybody agreed about Samir. Hugh looked at the other teachers discussing 8D's reports at the staff meeting. "He's actually very bright," he said bitterly. That morning, he'd had serious discipline problems with Samir again.

"His marks aren't bad," Nadia pointed out.

"But his behaviour leaves a lot to be desired," said Madame Dupond, the French teacher.

"He's a nasty piece of work!" Hugh was starting to lose his temper.

The room went quiet. The two class representatives, Sebastian and Nouria, were waiting for the verdict. Was Samir in trouble or not?

"We mustn't be too negative," said Mrs Cure, the tiny maths teacher, in a squeaky voice. "He's got 4 in geometry, and 5 in algebra." She pointed to Samir's scores in her register with a biro.

Nadia could tell her beloved Hugh was at breaking point. She was worried he'd explode and say he'd had it up to here with that kid. "We could put 'diswuptive influence'," she suggested.

Everybody around the table knew Samir's parents would sign his report without caring what "disruptive influence" meant.

"Good idea," they all agreed.

Except for Hugh, who started doodling on a piece of paper.

"Right, OK ... let's move on to Aisha," said Madame Dupond. "Oh, and let's talk about Nouria while we're at it."

The teachers smiled. Nouria winced.

"You have to understand, Nouria, we weren't born yesterday."

8D's girl representative decided to play it cool. "Why? Wassup?"

"What's up is, you two cheat all the time,"

Nadia pointed out. "Technically we ought to divide your avewage mark in half."

"That would make 0.5 in spelling," said Hugh.

The teachers tittered. Nouria shot him a filthy look. Aisha was the one who always copied from her. But she'd never give her friend away.

"Let's look on the bright side," squeaked Mrs Cure. "They've got 3 in geometry, which is a mark better than last term."

"They've got better at cheating," commented Madame Dupond. "I suppose it's some kind of progress. So, what are we putting on Aisha's report?"

Nouria was shaking. Not for herself. For Aisha. She looked down.

"Aisha's dad is a bit overprotective," the other representative said suddenly.

All eyes turned to Sebastian. He was a good-looking, kind, talented kid who was branded a geek by everybody in 8D.

"What are you trying to say?" Madame Dupond asked gently.

"Well ... *that*."

Sebastian wasn't going to let on that Aisha often

got slapped. She'd told him about being blasted once, because she'd needed him to write her book report.

The teachers didn't push him. They were only too aware that a number of their students had difficult home situations.

"We could put 'Aisha must make more of a personal effort'," suggested a squeaky voice.

Everybody admired the subtlety of this comment.

"A *personal* effort, spot on!"

"And as for the 1 in spelling, Mr Mullins, is there any way…"

"Oh, just give her a 5!" said Hugh airily.

The others tut-tutted. Hugh really hadn't got the hang of things yet.

"We don't want to discourage the children," came the squeaky voice again. "We can highlight their plus points without lying to them."

"How about 3 then?" Hugh suggested, feeling increasingly isolated.

Nadia wanted to throw her arms around him and tell him it was OK. But this wasn't the place for a hug.

"I've got Majid next," Madame Dupond went

on. "Who'd like to say something about Majid?"

Hugh opened his mouth, but Mrs Cure got there first.

"Now *he* definitely needs shaking up. He's got everything going for him. Delightful mother. Great dad. And he's a bright child. But he never make a blind bit of effort. Either in class or when it comes to homework."

This was the toughest attack so far. It sounded like Majid might have to stay down next year. Calimero's heart was racing.

"Well, that's ... um ... er ... unbelievable!" he stammered. "I've never had ... er ... any problems with him. None whatsoever!"

"Oh, come off it, he's always mucking about," said Madame Dupond.

"How? Like what?" protested Hugh, sounding as indignant as Mamadou.

"And he's only got 2 in geometry and 3 in algebra."

Hugh looked as if he was about to make Mrs Cure eat her register.

Things are hotting up, thought Nadia. She suggested, "'Must pull himself together next term if he wants to avoid wepeating the year.'"

"Good idea. He needs a warning," everybody agreed.

After the meeting, Hugh was walking home past Hummingbird Tower when he suddenly felt the urge to warn Majid. The reports were going out at the beginning of the following week, and Majid's mum was in for a big shock. She was convinced Majid was working hard.

Emmay was more than happy to welcome Mr Teacher back.

"It looks different in here," Hugh said. "Have you done something to the living room?"

"Iz new wallpaper!" said Mrs Badach proudly.

Hugh didn't like to laugh at people, but he couldn't help smirking when he saw Babar the Elephant all over the wall. Majid understood straight away and wanted to explain.

"Dad hasn't realized I've grown up."

"Iz true. Always he iz working, his father," Mrs Badach agreed. "And Majid, he try littel harder for skool? I say him, work, work!"

Hugh smiled faintly. He didn't have the heart to

tell her the truth. Majid's report was going to hurt her.

"Have you got any further with the game?" Majid asked point-blank.

Calimero instantly forgot why he'd come to the Badachs'. His eyes sparkled. "I've completed my first mission," he crowed, tucking his thumbs into his belt.

"Respect!"

"How about you?"

"I went to Golem City."

Majid had chosen the two doors on the left.

"I make littel tea? You like, Mr Mullins?"

"That'd be great, thanks, Mrs Badach," said Hugh, sitting down in front of Magic Berber's computer.

"D'you know what a golem is?" asked Majid.

"Er … it's a character in a Jewish tale, isn't it? A kind of Frankenstein story?"

"I found a website that explains it all."

Magic Berber pushed Calimero over and sat down in front of the computer. He typed rapidly, and they waited a few seconds. The site came up.

Golem: the golem is a being in human form created by magic. According to legend, making a golem involves taking a small pile of virgin clay and moulding it into the desired shape. Then the word EMET, meaning "truth" in Hebrew, has to be written...

While Hugh was reading this last sentence, the computer started crackling. The screen went red and an image, grey and hazy at first, replaced the text.

"Golem," Calimero and Magic Berber whispered.

Once again the computer was being hijacked by the game.

Enter your name.

Mrs Badach had come back into the living room. She glanced absent-mindedly at the screen. Majid had just typed **Magic Berber** on the scroll.

"Iz your tea, Mr Mullins," she said, putting a small steaming glass near the keyboard.

The screen opened up to reveal a corridor paved with black and white marble.

"Try the second door on the right," Hugh recommended.

"Yeah? What is it?"

But Calimero didn't tell him about the little warrior getting burnt to a cinder by the dragon. "Go on," he said again, trying not to laugh.

Majid made the little warrior move forward and then turn, before pressing ENTER. But nothing happened.

"Press!"

"What d'you think I'm doing?" Majid complained, pounding the ENTER key.

Calimero had a go too. The door wouldn't open.

"Leave it," said Majid. "Try the second door on the left."

Calimero smiled. "I smell a trap."

The little warrior entered a hangar full of piled-up crates. Behind the crates, mafia types in trilbies were playing cards. Two others, standing guard, instantly machine-gunned the little warrior.

Majid laughed. "What kind of welcome is that?"

But Hugh was thoughtful. When Majid had tried to go into the dragon's den, the command had been blocked. Once you'd given your player's name, you were only allowed to go in one direction.

The screen flashed:

Gunned down!
➤ start play
➤ end play

Magic Berber started again. He grabbed a machine gun in the first room to mow down the mafia types in the second, where a blue and gold motorbike was waiting.

"Full throttle!" shouted Majid.

The motorbike thundered off on a terrifying journey along winding mountain roads. The jolts, bends and precipices were so realistic they made Hugh feel sick. A map appeared in a corner of the screen. Majid didn't bother with the magnifying glass but clicked instantly on Golem City.

Majid was already an expert. He'd got a long way into the game in previous sessions, further than Hugh with Golemia. He'd outsmarted all the traps and entered the heart of Golem City. It was an incredible place – grimy and futuristic at the same time.

Majid knew all the game's sleazy dives and opium dens. The little warrior drove around on his motorbike talking to everybody: tramps, posh types and gangsters. Half rude-boy, half old-fashioned knight, he collected weapons, first-aid kits and rolls of dollars in his bottomless pockets. Hugh was full of admiration as he watched Majid do his stuff. They leant against each other, laughing and shouting. They looked like brothers, noticed Mrs Badach, becoming emotional. She thought about Majid's six brothers, especially Haziz, who she hadn't heard from for a long time. She shook her head to shrug off her sadness.

The screen flashed:

To find out what your third mission is, type EME.

Majid followed the instruction and the little warrior, still with his visor down, found himself standing by a lift on the ground floor.

"This is Golem's Victory, the tallest building in Golem City," Majid explained. "There are one hundred and seventy-two floors. I thought I was going to lose it, man. There are tons of traps. I got killed four times."

But the more he'd explored, the more Magic

Berber had realized that the seventh floor was the only one worth accessing. "It's not hard to remember," he said. "I'm the seventh son…"

"So I'd be better off on the first floor," joked Hugh. "I'm an only child."

"Yeah? At least you didn't get any hassle."

They were following the little warrior's movements on the screen as they talked. A hand appeared over the door to room 777, inviting them to click on it.

"Your call," said Majid, pushing the mouse towards Hugh.

The door opened. They were in an empty hotel room.

"So what are we meant to do?" Hugh asked.

"Search me. I spent half an hour trying to figure it out the other evening. No traps, no enemies. Nothing to collect. I don't get it."

Hugh moved the cursor across the screen. There was nobody in the room, but a guest had left behind a suitcase, a scattering of clothes and a half-empty glass.

"What's that?" Hugh asked, pointing to a corner of the screen.

There was a white blob at the foot of the bed. A big pile of pixels.

"It's a bug," Majid answered.

They fell silent, anxious almost, scouring the screen for clues.

"I don't get it either," Hugh said at last.

The little warrior seemed to agree. He'd frozen with his back to them and his machine gun idle.

Suddenly the screen misted over. Hugh and Majid were almost relieved. There's nothing worse than a riddle without an answer.

"Right," Hugh said dreamily.

"Right," Majid echoed.

They were giddy from playing for so long.

"Crikey, it's eight o'clock," Calimero panicked. "I didn't tell my mu— Er ... I'm off. Goodbye, Mrs Badach."

Getting home would have been much quicker on Bubble's back, he thought, especially since the lift in Hummingbird Tower was out of order again.

That night, Hugh turned the mystery of room 777 over and over in his head. At about one o'clock in the morning, he had an idea. The pile of pixels.

Yes, that was it. But he fell asleep before he got to wherever his hunch was taking him.

Back at Hummingbird Tower, Emmay dreamt Haziz was calling out to her for help. And Magic Berber spent half the night riding his motorbike.

But nobody, not a single person, either in their dreams or in real life, saw the little cloud of smoke coming out of the Badachs' flat.

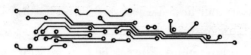

Golem-Okh

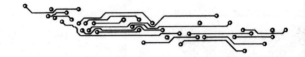

The next morning, Mrs Badach woke up with heartache. The kind of heartache people get when they've been through a lot, and suffered a lot too. All those boys, *so many* sons. Bringing them up hadn't been easy... Now and then they remembered to telephone her. But they had their own lives to lead. She understood. And so, while she was busy preparing the kebabs for Majid's supper, Emmay kept telling herself she *was* happy.

Suddenly she tuned into a noise that'd been coming from the living room for a while.

"Majid?"

But her son was at school.

Mrs Badach stuck her head round the kitchen door. Nobody. She could hear a noise, though, like paper being crumpled or an insect buzzing. Probably just some repair work being carried out in the building. She got back to her kebabs.

The noise was close by now. And it really was coming from the living room. Not the corridor or the neighbours. Emmay wasn't easily frightened. But she'd had a bad dream last night and she believed in dreams.

"Haziz?"

For a moment she was sure there was somebody on the other side of the door, and she thought of her son who'd disappeared. She went back into the living room. The Babars on the wallpaper looked harmless enough in their handsome green suits. But the noise was definitely coming from somewhere within those four walls.

At Moreland School, Hugh was writing his reports in the staffroom. But his thoughts were somewhere else. He was trying to work out the mystery of room 777. It *had* to be Golem's bug that was holding them back. The pile of pixels was clearly hiding something. If Golem had been for sale in the shops, Hugh would have taken it back. But the game only existed on the Net. So who were you meant to complain to?

"Hi, Thugh!"

Hugh looked up and gave Nadia a winning smile without even realizing it. He'd just remembered the hunch he'd had the night before. He was *that* close to finding the answer. The white blob. The third mission. What was the fourth? The golem… He'd read something about golems at Majid's.

"Have you come across the golem legend?" he asked.

Nadia tried to look like she thought this was a perfectly normal question to be asked in the staffroom at 10.05 a.m. "Is that what you're working on in class?"

"No."

Nadia swallowed a sigh. He really was weird. "I think it was a kind of monthter."

"Yes. Created out of a pile of—" Hugh's jaw dropped and his eyes glazed over. A pile of pixels!

"A pile of clay," said Nadia, finishing his sentence.

Hugh skipped lunch in the canteen and ran all the way home. He wanted to revisit Majid's website about golems.

> Then the word EMET, meaning "truth" in Hebrew, has to be written on the golem's forehead in order to give it life. When the first letter is erased, the word MET is left, meaning "death", and the golem becomes nothing again.

You had to type E to get hold of the dragon or the motorbike. To enter Golemia or Golem City, you typed EM. Majid had carried out his third mission by typing EME. Which meant that only the letter T was missing before truth would appear: EMET. Majid was nearly there. Hugh's hunch from the night before was fast becoming a reality. He typed:

<Calimero> As soon as you're in the game again, go back to room 777. Type the letters EMET and click on the pile of pixels. It's not a bug. It's a golem.

Majid walked back to Hummingbird Tower with Samir after school that day. Somewhere in his mind, Majid was scared of his new friend. But he was flattered too.

"Emmay, akli dhe gueham!"

Emmay appeared in the kitchen doorway. She looked tired.

"What's wrong?" asked her son, who noticed more than he let on.

"Iz work in building. Maybe they iz doing again electricals."

"About time. Everything's brucked around here."

Majid peered at his computer screen and read the message from Calimero.

"What's that?" asked Samir, intrigued by what looked like some kind of code.

For a split second, Magic Berber held back. Then he told Samir everything. How Calimero was their English teacher. How they'd found a wicked game on the Net. How a golem was a bit like Frankenstein's monster. Samir kept blinking and frowning and saying "Oh yeah?" He could barely contain his jealousy. He wanted to have this computer, to play this game, to take Majid's place.

"So how d'you play Golem?" he asked casually.

"That's the problem. It hijacks the network. You can't just play it when you want to."

Samir liked the sound of a pirate game. Maybe it was a trial version of something soon to be released. "You know what? We could make a copy of it. My cousin's got a CD-writer." Samir had all sorts of cousins with all sorts of expensive gizmos. "It could make lots of babies."

"And we could sell them!" Majid was getting carried away.

"Nah? Really?" Samir teased. "We'll make nuff dollars. You could buy a moped." He winked. "And treat Aisha too."

Majid glanced over his shoulder.

"No worries, your old lady's out of range," Samir reassured him.

Majid pretended to laugh. But he only half liked this kind of talk.

"Hey, isn't that your game?" Samir asked suddenly, his eyes on the screen.

Majid shivered. Yes! It was Golem. The game had spontaneously installed itself.

Samir grabbed the mouse. "How does it work?"

Majid panicked. "Wait, hold on." It had just sunk in that he'd given away a secret. Samir was going to steal some of the mystery. The game flashed up:

Enter your name.

Samir typed his name.

"No," Magic Berber objected, "you're not supposed to put your real name."

"Why not?" Samir ignored him and pressed ENTER. "I had a go on my cousin's computer."

"Yeah, but this game isn't like that."

"Like what?"

Up on the screen came:

Choose your weapon, Samir!

"Why's the M underlined?"

"I don't know," Majid lied.

"Geek," said Samir scornfully, pressing M.

Four strange-looking weapons appeared in the left-hand corner of the screen. They were baroque matchlocks, guns from another era. Samir chose one with a spike on the end. When the little warrior started his training, the spike flew off with a high-pitched whistling noise. It was attached to the gun by a rope, making an awesome harpoon. The spike disappeared. They heard a dull thud followed by a horrible cry, and then blood trickled down the screen.

Samir laughed ferociously. "Nasty!"

The screen said:

To find out what your first mission is, type E.

The warrior was advancing at a rapid pace and the game was speeding up. Majid went quiet. Samir was gloating.

"Which door d'you reckon?" he asked in the marble-paved corridor.

"Second on the left," Majid suggested. He was waiting for Samir to get gunned down.

But the command was blocked and Samir couldn't open the door.

"Da-aa-mm! This game's got a bug!"

"Samir, you spik Inglish proper!" Mrs Badach shouted from the kitchen.

"Whoops, sorry, Mrs Badach. Won't say *bug* again."

"I know you thinking you iz more smart than everybody," retorted Emmay. "But life, it iz more smart than you."

"And Golem, it iz more strong than you, innit!" mimicked Samir. "OK, what am I doing here? How about the third door?"

He didn't wait for an answer. The door opened onto a moonlit cemetery. There was no time for him to make sense of what was going on. The little warrior took one step, but it was one too many. A horrible beast had been waiting in ambush at the top of the screen. It came crashing down onto the warrior's back and clung to him, sinking its teeth into his neck.

"Ah, ma-aa-an!" Samir shouted, pressing the trigger of his harpoon gun. But the weapon was useless because the vampire was on the warrior's back.

"Shame," Majid gloated.

The screen was triumphant too:

Made you bleed!
➤ start play
➤ end play

"You've got to start with the right-hand door."

"Nah? Really?"

Mrs Badach placed two steaming glasses of mint tea near the boys. She glanced at the screen. She didn't understand computers, and she was mystified as to how they were supposed to make you clever.

Samir opened the door on the right and the little warrior entered a chapel. A crucifix decorated with a garland of garlic towered over the altar. On either side, a pair of gargoyles contemplated their destiny.

"Steer clear of the gargoyles," warned Majid.

"Nah? Really?" This had become Samir's catchphrase. He pulled the trigger, snared the crucifix with his harpoon and dragged it towards him. "Me tellin' ya, man, is like da good medicine 'gainst da vampire," he said in a voodoo accent.

Sure enough, as soon as it saw the crucifix, the vampire prostrated itself at the little warrior's feet. The warrior climbed onto its back and rose up into the sky.

The sky turned out to be full of bats and witches.

A graveyard with gaping tombs gave way first to a dismal quarry haunted by women in white, then to a heath where a horse with empty eye sockets roamed around. Worst of all was the soundscape of squeakings, groanings and whinnyings.

"This game's nasty!" Samir was on a high, like somebody drinking blood.

An old map appeared. It was half burnt, but Majid and Samir could just make out the name of the capital: Golem-Okh.

A spell had been cast over Golem-Okh. It was always night there. Every door turned into a portcullis as soon as the warrior approached. Every staircase disappeared into nothingness. Samir died five times, getting impaled and having his head blown to smithereens. The blood was so realistic and gory it looked stuck to the screen.

"We're gonna make nuff dollars out of this game!" exclaimed Samir, rubbing his hands together.

When he finally escaped the ghosts and ghouls of Golem-Okh, he found himself in front of a castle with towers and crenellations more intricate than a piece of lace. A greenish light glowed in every window. The little warrior was heavily armed from his previous battles. No pallid ghosts or pointy-toothed butlers could stop him now. He explored the castle, and then made his way down into the dungeons.

"What happens next?"

A skeleton was chained to the wall. Close by lay a dead rat and an old broken jar. Nothing to take, nothing to kill, nowhere to go. Samir tried making the skeleton talk by moving the warrior over to it and pressing the space bar. Nothing.

"Look, there's a joker in your game," he pointed out.

It was a white blob, just like the pile of pixels in room 777.

"Wait, we've got to do what Calimero said!"

"Calimero," sniggered Samir.

Majid typed **EMET**. Truth. Would it reveal itself? He positioned the arrow over the bug and clicked. Nothing.

"Try the other button on the mouse," Samir suggested.

Click.

The pile of pixels quivered. Slowly it began to take shape, flaring out towards the top as if moulded by an invisible potter. Slowly, silently, words appeared:

Here is your golem, master.

Thanks, Bubble!

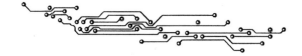

Mrs Mullins wasn't easily frightened. But there'd been a strange noise in the flat all afternoon and it was getting on her nerves. It was like the buzzing under electricity pylons. Or an insect sizzling to death on a light bulb. She got several small shocks from the window latches, and her flyaway hair had become unmanageable, crackling between her fingers when she tried to control it. Eventually she hit on the idea of airing the flat, and the fresh breeze swept away the static electricity.

When she closed the windows, she noticed the noise had stopped. She carried on with her sewing, feeling much calmer now. She was making a skirt for the spring. Suddenly she turned round.

"Hugh?"

But her son wouldn't be back until later. Dreamily, Mrs Mullins picked up her thread, and her thoughts. Living alone with a grown-up son wasn't easy. Alone? She gave a start. It felt like there was somebody right behind her.

"Harvey?"

Her husband had been dead for more than ten years. So why had she called out his name? Mrs Mullins wasn't easily frightened. But that was exactly how she felt right now. No other word for it.

"I'll go for a walk," she said out loud.

It did her good. She sighed with relief when she got back. Hugh was home early for some reason. She could hear him working in his study.

"Have you eaten, Hugh?" She opened the study door. "Hugh…"

She nearly shrieked. There was nobody there. She could have sworn she'd heard something a moment earlier. A sound like pieces of paper being scrunched up.

Hugh took his time getting home. He'd had to teach 8D last class. Miguel had brought along the latest craze: Big B farting goo. It was a cross between Silly Putty and a whoopee cushion. If you worked the goo between your fingers, you produced variations on a favourite theme, triggering comments like "Nice one!" and "Who's let off a stinker?"

Hugh hadn't been able to intercept the tub of goo as it changed hands around the class. But Magic Berber had dropped it when it got to him, and Calimero had picked it up.

"Have you seen what I confiscated off 8D?" Hugh was laughing, happy as a twelve-year-old with his new toy.

"Ah, there you are!" exclaimed Mrs Mullins, as if her son had just got back from cod fishing in the North Sea.

"Yeah...?" He looked at his mother, surprised. She'd always mollycoddled him, but this was getting beyond a joke.

Mrs Mullins couldn't explain the terrible time she'd been having. It was ... unexplainable. Very faint noises, the feeling there was somebody there, static electricity in the door handles... Nothing concrete, no evidence. And everything was back to normal now.

"I ... I'm going to do some work," Hugh mumbled.

In his study he threw his jacket over his swivel chair and put the farting goo on top of a pile of exercise books he had to mark. He made a mental note to buy some goo for his next-door neighbour's little girl as well as for his mother's godson. Then he sat down in front of the computer. There was a message waiting for him.

<Magic_Berber> I done wot u sed about the tarsk and your rite its the golem. Its horible it doesnt even have a face. I cant realy explane it. You gota see. But samir messt up the game...

Samir? Hugh was horrified. What had Samir got to do with it? And how had he messed up?

He had no time to find out. Golem had just installed itself on his screen again, like an old friend who happened to be passing.

"Golem," said Hugh, imitating the game's deep voice.

He'd got into the habit of saving his sessions now. In no time, he was back in Golemia.

On previous attempts Hugh had dodged the archers' arrows and his dragon had been able to land on a flat roof. In order to make a low-key entrance into the city, the little warrior had entrusted Bubble to an old woman in exchange for the flask. But he'd been ambushed and the city guards had taken him prisoner. Hugh had rubbed the lamp to make the genie appear and free the little warrior. After escaping, he had used his compass to move all over Golemia and collect weapons and life points.

Today he was standing in front of a palace straight out of The Thousand and One Nights. It was all locked up and, as luck would have it, the only object the warrior hadn't used for his missions yet was the key. There were three locked doors. A magnificent dragon was carved on the first one, which looked like it was made of bronze. Hugh thought of Bubble and fancied his chances. But he moved on to the second door all the same. It glistened like gold and, since the key was also golden, he had almost made up his mind. Just to be on the safe side, he took a look at the third door. It was wooden and plain, apart from the number 111.

Hugh knew he had to make a decision before the game disappeared again. He was convinced the white blob was behind one of these doors.

"The golden door?" he whispered.

He moved the cursor. Just as he was about to click on it, he remembered room 777, where Majid's golem was. They'd joked about it, because Majid was the seventh son and Hugh was an only child.

"111…"

It was stupid. There was no way the game's programmers could know Hugh was the only Mullins child. But the more Calimero played Golem, the more he believed in the game's unusual powers. He clicked on door 111 and the little warrior was blown back by an explosion.

"No!"

The red life bar had halved. Another mistake like that, and he'd have to find the old lady with the warrior's healing flask.

"OK. Let's try the dragon."

Hugh clicked on the first door and the chiselled dragon flew off with a cry. The door opened.

"Thanks, Bubble!"

Hugh didn't know what to expect, and there was nothing special about the room he'd just entered. A four-poster bed, a chest, a fire in the hearth. He typed **EMET**. Then he moved the cursor around the screen. There was an ugly white blob on an oriental rug. He positioned the arrow over it and left-clicked. Nothing. Right-click.

The pile of pixels quivered. Slowly it began to take shape, flaring out towards the top as if moulded by an invisible potter. Slowly, silently, words appeared:

Here is your golem, master.

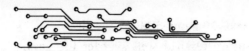

I've Got to Have My Golem!

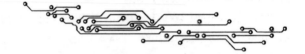

Majid had a sinking feeling when he saw the shape-less golem. Part white clay, part flashing pixels, the creature had a hole instead of a mouth, its eyes looked stitched on its floppy flesh and it had no nostrils to speak of. Its wrinkled, saggy, anaemic body was bent over in a grotesque bow. It spoke in a deep voice and it chewed its words.

"I am your golem, master."

"Sexy," sneered Samir. "He'll have all the girls falling for him."

But what fell was the cup of mint tea Mrs Badach had put dangerously close to the keyboard. Samir knocked it as he greeted the golem.

"Are you crazy?" shouted Majid angrily.

The hot sugary tea had spilt all over the keys, killing the keyboard and paralysing the computer. The image of the golem bowing was stuck on the screen for ever. To protect what was left of his machine, Majid turned it off.

"Are you mental?" he shouted again, thumping Samir with surprising force.

"Nah, you are!"

The two boys landed on the carpet. Mrs Badach ran in, getting hit as she tried to break them up.

"Majid, Majid, think of your father!" she sobbed. She caught her son round the waist, separating him from his opponent.

Samir stood up and wiped blood from his nose. "He's mad," he gasped. "It's only the keyboard, Mrs Badach. My cousins can get him another one."

"Yes, you see, you find other keyboard," said Mrs Badach, her voice choked with emotion. "Iz no big deal, Majid. I buy you other one. Iz no big deal…" She was almost cradling him.

"It's on the house, Mrs Badach. A freebie, you get me?" Samir insisted. "My cousins can sort it out, no problem."

His brain was working overtime, hatching a plan. To get his own back on Majid and his stupid friend Calimero. To make that idiot pay for punching him.

Pay big time.

"You see?" said Emmay. "Samir he get it from Mister Fribee, friend of cousin. Iz no big deal. Iz not nice idea to fight, Majid. Always there iz other way."

"Yeah, right." Majid was livid. He was on the verge of tears. "But I can't play any more. I was about to get my golem and now I won't. And it's all this loser's fault." It made him feel better to call Samir a loser. He took a deep breath.

Samir didn't bat an eyelid. "Iz no big deal, Majid." He chuckled as he left the flat. "I've found the *other way*."

When Hugh saw his own golem for the first time, he didn't know what had gone on at Majid's. But he understood what Magic Berber meant about the golem being a faceless creature. The invisible potter wasn't big on details. After widening the base and narrowing the neck, he or she had just rolled a head and made two or three knife marks on it for the face. The eyes were dreadful. They looked like they were sewn up round the edges with cross-stitches that dug into the floppy flesh. The shapeless golem bowed to its master.

"Hey, fatso!" Hugh welcomed it. "I reckon you've got a way to go before we're seen in public together."

"I am your golem. Make me the way you would like me to be," the golem answered in a fuzzy voice.

The old typewriter starting rattling the screen again, and Hugh read:

To make your golem, type E.

"Here we go," he whispered as he pressed E.

Enter your golem's name.

He paused a second to snigger at the clumsy pallid blob that was waddling about, waiting for its master to make up his mind.

What if my golem was a girl-golem? Hugh thought. I bet the programmers didn't think of that.

As soon as he wrote **Natasha** on the scroll, an identification sheet rolled down the screen:

eye colour
hair colour
skin colour
length and style of hair
height
weight
vital statistics
eye shape
nose shape
mouth shape
chin shape
forehead shape
ear shape
jawline
eyebrow arch
distinguishing marks or features

"Wow!" exclaimed Hugh. "What's... But I don't..." He was completely blown away. It felt like all the girls in the world were suddenly throwing themselves at his feet. He stood up and shouted, "Mum!"

He rushed into the sitting room, giving Mrs Mullins, who was still working on her sewing, a shock.

"What's the matter?"

"D'you … d'you know Lara Croft's vital statistics?"

"Lara Croft…"

"Yeah, or a supermodel's. What's the perfect figure?"

Being a psychologist, Mrs Mullins knew that mothers must be tactful in these situations. If Hugh suddenly needed to know the ideal vital statistics for a girl, it wasn't her business to ask why.

"Er, well, um, I think 36–24–34 is pretty good."

"Thirty-six?" he repeated suspiciously. "Is that enough?"

"Er, well, um, I think it's ample…" She laughed a bit and stammered in her embarrassment. "No, I promise, it's … it's plenty to be getting on with."

Hugh nodded and went back into his study, closing the door behind him. His mother didn't know whether to get her hopes up or start worrying.

Calimero sat in front of his computer again and began to fill out Natasha's identification sheet. He was all fired up. He typed in the most important bit first: 36–24–34.

The golem appeared in the space opposite, and the invisible potter sculpted energetically.

"Is that it?" asked Hugh, taken aback.

A completely different shape was emerging, with plenty of curves, but still cloud textured. For *eye colour* Hugh barely paused before writing *green*. The poor golem's stitched eyes came out dark green.

"Not great," he muttered, and changed it to *light green*. Then he got carried away: *with gold specks when it's sunny and dark glints when it rains*. An amazing palette of colours popped up, and he chose a soft green tinged with golden flecks. He settled down comfortably in his chair. He was going to be there a while. An array of shades popped up for the hair colour.

"No contest: *strawberry blonde*... That's it? Yuck!"

The pasty golem was starting to look increasingly absurd with its mop of tousled hair and its green cross-stitched eyes.

Next he wanted to remedy his golem's floury complexion.

"OK, *pale tan* it is. I don't like girls who fry themselves in the sun, but right now, darling, you look peaky."

The cloud had become flesh-like as it was compressed. Now it had a delicate suntan too. The possibilities of this game made Hugh feel giddy.

"Right, let's pop to the hairdresser's!"

He chose a plait with a fringe. Then he changed his mind and asked for loose shoulder-length hair. "*Wavy, but not too wavy.* Let's see. No, I prefer the plait." He kept plaiting and unplaiting his creation before he hit on the answer. She could have a plait in the daytime, and let her hair flow loose over the pillow at night.

"Height. Hold on, I'm five foot ten and I don't want to look a midget next to her. So *five foot seven* and *nine and a half stone* for the weight. I don't want a bag of bones either. OK?"

But the end product was still a long way off. The more feminine the golem became, the more alarming its featureless face looked.

"No worries, babe. Let's try a spot of cosmetic surgery. I'm going to give you *large, slightly almond-shaped eyes.* Forget the cross-stitches. And *long silky lashes.* You'll be drop-dead gorgeous by the time I've finished. Now … what about your nose?"

He was talking to the screen – or so it seemed.

"Straight, hey? We'll give you a classic nose, but we'll keep it small. And your mouth?"

He thought about it for a long time. Mouths mattered. Big? Fleshy lips? Ouch, she'd look like a man-eater… Thin and deep red? She'd look like Cruella de Vil. He made up his mind. *Shapely, quite full, hint of lipstick.*

He asked for a chin that was *round, well defined and not double.* And a forehead that was *smooth and intelligent.* Small ears, well-formed cheeks with high cheekbones and arched eyebrows completed the look. Sometimes the computer simplified his requests, but it did what he asked.

Hugh spent a good five minutes admiring Natasha. "Perfect!" he whispered. He glanced round to make sure the door between him and his mother was properly closed, before adding another two inches to the bust. He let out a wolf whistle.

But Natasha was about as sexy as a mannequin in a shop window. She was missing that certain something all girls have, whether they've got gold-green eyes and strawberry blonde hair or not. So Hugh added:

distinguishing features: she's a REAL babe!

Natasha immediately popped up dressed in a tiny pair of shorts and a strappy top. She blew a kiss and froze, hands on hips, looking rebellious and gorgeous at the same time.

"Wow … wow … wow…"

Hugh was speechless. He'd wear a hole in the screen if he carried on staring at it like that.

"Hugh! Telephone!" called Mrs Mullins, poking her head round the door.

"Huh?"

"Phone. Your girlfriend."

"What girlfriend?" Hugh couldn't take his eyes off the screen.

"You know, Nadia the science teacher!" said his exasperated mother. "Aren't you going to speak to her?"

Hugh pouted like a petulant kid. He'd tell Nadia where to go. But as soon as he stood up, Natasha disappeared.

"My golem!"

Samir Plays His Cards Right

It would soon be the Easter holidays. 8D had got their reports, the head had congratulated Sebastian, and Aisha's dad had dished out the slaps.

"What about your mum?" Hugh asked Majid.

"What d'you mean?" said Majid, going into head-butt mode.

"What did she say about your report?"

"Nothing."

"She didn't mind?"

"She can't read English, can she?"

Hugh was shocked and didn't really understand. "But you must have read out the bit about staying down a year?"

"No point. I'll catch up. I'm not doing that, no way."

They were in the classroom after the end of lessons. They didn't bother keeping their friendship secret any more.

"What are you going to do about your keyboard?" Calimero wanted to know. He hadn't said anything yet, but he'd be more than happy to give Magic Berber one as a present.

"I'm getting another on Saturday," said Majid, looking away. "OK, I'm out of here. Talk on the network on Sunday?"

Calimero smiled. "I've got a few things to fill you in on." He hadn't told Majid about Natasha. Or the fluorescent farting goo he'd found at Big B Stores. Special offer. Four tubs for the price of two.

Samir had promised Majid a free keyboard. But Samir's cousins had an unusual way of getting hold of computer supplies, so Majid didn't want grownups involved. Especially not Calimero.

Samir had arranged to meet Majid on Saturday evening in the basements of Hummingbird Tower.

And he'd said, "*Freebies* rhymes with *nobody sees*. You get me?"

At seven o'clock, Majid was confusing his mum with a story about one of Samir's cousins passing by the estate with a spare keyboard. Mrs Badach thought it was too late to be knocking on neighbours' doors.

"I'll only be gone ten minutes!" Before his mum could say anything, Majid grabbed his jacket and tore down twelve flights of stairs.

Normally the basements of Hummingbird Tower were locked. Stuff had gone on down there: raves that had turned nasty, fights between different crews. None of the tenants stored anything down there any more and the main entrance had been padlocked. But the padlock had disappeared this evening, and Majid was able to sneak inside. He immediately thought of Golem City, with its secret opium dens and sleazy dives. He wanted to click on 5 to recover his machine gun.

Samir had promised Majid he'd be waiting in his parents' lot, number 312, and from there they'd go together to meet his cousin in a nearby lot. It had all seemed straightforward at the time. And Samir had been very insistent. But now, as Majid made his way through the basements, counting the numbers on the doors – 309, 310 – he sensed there was something dodgy about their arrangement.

"Samir!"

The timer-switch crackled, threatening to plunge Majid into darkness. Lot 311 … 312. The door was ajar.

"Samir?"

But Majid already knew nobody else was going to turn up to this meeting. Nobody? He jumped. It was that stupid crackling from the timer-switch. Time to head back.

That was when he realized he'd been tricked. He could hear voices coming from the main entrance. Men's voices. He had no choice but to go deeper into the basements. What was he meant to say if they found him in a place that was strictly out of bounds? Oddly enough, he wasn't scared, even though the men were hot on his heels. He could hear what they were saying.

"This way?"

"No, straight ahead. It's in 312. That's what the lad said on the phone."

Majid wasn't scared because he'd turned into the helmeted warrior. Space bar: *toc, toc, toc*, straight ahead. c: down on all fours. Left arrow: turn left. The light was broken. It was pitch black, but darkness protects you from the enemy. The voices were close now.

"Look!" said one of the men triumphantly. "They've left a whole pile of stuff. Grab that, it's a car radio. And what's that, over there? Another radio."

Majid crouched down behind a box.

"OK, we'd better put the padlock back," said the other man.

The padlock? Majid would be locked in. He wanted to stand up and shout, "Wait, I'm turning myself in!" But his warrior's pride made him bite his lips till they bled.

The footsteps were further off now.

"You going to tell the police?" asked one of the men.

The police? I'd rather starve to death! thought Majid, still huddled behind the box. In a flash he saw his brother Haziz the day of his arrest. For handling a few jacked mopeds. He remembered how upset Emmay had been, how ashamed his dad was, the neighbours on the landing. No, not that, never again.

Cramp in his calf muscle made him stand up. And that was when he got a real fright.

A white shape floated past the end of the corridor. At the same time, all the basement lots were plunged into darkness.

"Can't you find the switch?" a voice shouted.

"I'm pressing, but nothing's happening!"

The shape had frozen. It was white and luminous in the dark, as if lit up from the inside.

Majid recognized it. Impossibly, he recognized it. It crackled and gave off blue sparks.

"Emmay!" shouted the little warrior.

Majid rushed towards the exit, colliding with the two men in the dark.

"What on earth…? Got him!" yelled one of the men. "So the lad on the phone was right. He told me these scumbags hang out in the basements at night."

Majid tried to break free, but it was no good.

The caretaker of Hummingbird Tower had him in a tight grip.

"Look at that vermin!" said the other. "How old d'you reckon? Ten?"

"Tell you what, I know who he is and all," said the caretaker. "He's the youngest Badach kid. I've lost count of them in that family. His mum's going to be one happy lady when she finds out."

"Therza ... therza..." stammered Majid in a state of shock. "A whi... A whi..."

The caretaker shook him. "Don't make out you can't understand English, sonny."

"But ... the gol— gol— gol..."

"Therza ... therza ... gol— gol..." The caretaker imitated him. "I can talk that Arab lingo too, sonny, with my foot up your backside!"

A pit of shame opened that Saturday and swallowed a twelve-year-old helmeted warrior. First there was the call from the caretaker to alert Emmay. Then the drive to the police station. The interrogation. The inspector's warning. Emmay crying. Mr Badach rushing over from work. The slap. The journey home in silence.

Majid had denied everything at the police station. No, he wasn't involved in handling stolen goods, least of all car radios that thieves didn't know what to do with.

"It's not me," he kept saying frantically. "It's Samir!"

"Who's Samir?" the inspector asked Mrs Badach.

"Iz friend, Mr Police."

Emmay wanted to leave it at that, and keep the shame to herself. But the inspector needed Samir's address and surname. He wanted to find out who was behind all this. The small boy in front of him was clearly not responsible for stealing the mound of gear stashed away in lot 312.

"It's Samir's lot," said Majid accusingly.

The inspector rang Samir's parents. No, it wasn't their lot. Theirs was number 108.

Majid knew the game was up. Nobody would believe him. No point even mentioning the meeting and the free keyboard. He'd only make things worse for himself.

As for telling them what he'd really seen down there, he was on dangerous ground. Only one person would believe him. Maybe. But Magic Berber couldn't contact Calimero any more, because Mr Badach had decided on his son's punishment.

"No more computer."

The news was all round Moreland School first thing Monday morning: Majid had gone to the police station because of something to do with stolen car radios. At lunchtime the educational psychologist had a word with Madame Dupond, who was responsible for the students' pastoral care, and who in turn told the head, who happened to run into Nadia that evening at Big B Stores.

By Tuesday morning Hugh had found out all about it.

"Why?"

Hugh and Majid were face to face. They'd waited until all the students slyly watching them had given up and left.

"Why'd you do it?"

"I didn't do anything. It was Samir. I could kill him."

Majid's voice was full of hatred, and it made him sound more grown up. Hugh winced.

"What're you talking about? Samir's got nothing to do with it."

"Yeah, right," said Majid glumly. "He knew there were loads of jacked car radios in that lot. He told me to meet him there and then tipped off the caretaker."

This explanation didn't make any sense to Hugh. "But why would Samir tell you to meet him in the basements?"

This was where Samir had played his cards right.

"He promised me a free keyboard," stammered Majid.

"A free keyboard? In the basements!" Hugh shook his head and sighed. Kids. The more they tried to explain the mess they were in, the less you understood. "This is ludicrous. I could have got you a keyboard without stealing it!" Seeing his friend on the verge of tears, he added, "I still can, by the way."

"There's no point." Majid looked up defiantly. "I'm not allowed to use the computer any more."

Silence. Calimero had just lost Magic Berber. The teacher held out his hand to his student.

"Leave it." Majid's voice wobbled. He looked

at the hand Calimero was offering him. Then he said fiercely, "I'll shake your hand when you believe me."

Majid could feel anger pumping through him as he walked out of school. He noticed Aisha waiting at the end of the road, her schoolbag between her legs. Aisha without Nouria. A rare sight. He didn't want to talk to her. But he didn't want to avoid her either, so he walked straight past.

"Majid!" she called out.

"What? I've got nothing to say to you." One more comment and he'd beat somebody up. But he needed to convince at least one person, so he added, "I didn't steal anything."

Aisha was embarrassed, and looked down. "It's not about that. It's about something I saw. Nouria doesn't believe me." She didn't have anybody else to tell her secret to. So when she saw Majid looking unhappy, her first thought was that at least he wouldn't make fun of her.

"Something you saw?"

They started walking side by side, hands in pockets. He was thinking about what he'd seen in the basements. She was thinking about what she'd seen near the Badachs' door.

"You won't tell anybody else?" Aisha made him promise.

Majid thought about it. What if they both had something to tell?

"Go on then," he said. "I've got a secret too. I'll tell you about it after."

You tell me yours, I'll tell you mine.

They whispered as they walked close together, their hands still in their pockets.

Aisha's secret was surprising.

Majid's was unbelievable.

Nice Cousins

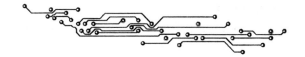

It didn't take Samir long to realize he'd have to pay for tricking Majid. Big time. The last Saturday of the holidays, when he was hanging around Hummingbird Tower, a battered old Volvo pulled up beside him.

"Get in," ordered the driver.

"*Please*," added a voice from the back. "Let's mind our Ps and Qs."

Samir had a very large extended Algerian family, including dozens of cousins. These two always stuck together, and they scared him. What did they want? No point trying to escape. They'd track him down on the estate. He got into the front seat.

"What's this about?" he asked, jerking his neck forward in head-butt mode.

"Forgotten how to say hello, have we?" said the voice in the back. "'Hello, Miloud. Hello, Rachid.'"

Rachid always spoke in a sickly-sweet voice. For some reason, it reminded Samir of a razor blade.

"Congratulations on the hideout," said Miloud as they drove off. "Great idea to take your friends there."

Samir frowned. His cousins clearly thought he'd overstepped the mark. "What? What hideout? I didn't do anything. Anyway, there was nothing in the basements." He knew they were talking about lot 312. But he also knew there was nothing in it except a pile of car radios they couldn't shift. "It's disused," he added.

"What d'you mean? Who's abused?" asked Miloud suspiciously. He and school had gone their separate ways early on.

Samir shrugged. "Disused," he repeated. "It means nobody's using it any more. All the lots in Hummingbird Tower are disused."

"You're not here to teach us to speak proper,

Samir," said Rachid. "The thing is, those basements come in ever so useful."

"Yeah," agreed Miloud. "We'd like to abuse them again, get it?"

"You're not meant to say—" But Samir stopped the grammar lesson mid-sentence. He'd just felt something at the top of his spine. It was sharp, it hurt and it was ready to dig in deeper. The Volvo was heading along an almost deserted B-road. He felt like he was in one of those Saturday night TV films, where the corpse tumbles out of the car door.

"What's in the basements?" he whispered.

"Gear," Miloud answered. "An order from a club-owner, all right?"

Rachid interrupted him. "No details."

"But the pigs didn't find anything apart from jacked car radios," Samir snivelled.

"I told you to be polite," Rachid warned him. "We don't say *pigs*, we say Feds, don't we? You got to clean up your act."

The blade had cut through Samir's jacket.

"You get me?"

"Yes, Rachid."

"Please, Samir," Rachid went on, "see how polite I'm asking you? Please would you go and get our gear for us? There's two grand's worth of stuff down there. Go and find it before our friends the police come back to abuse the basements."

"You've got two days," Miloud added. "It's in 401."

He gave Samir instructions on how to find the precious packet. Then he did a quick U-turn and slammed on the brakes. In the distance the towers of the Moreland Estate rose up into the dull grey sky.

"See what nice guys we are. We're dropping you off in the right direction."

Samir realized he'd have to walk back. Now that the car had come to a stop, he peeled himself off the seat and turned to face Rachid. "Why don't *you* go down there?" he asked. "It's your stuff, not mine."

"You've got people looking at the basements now," Rachid answered. "It's not going to be easy. The caretaker's keeping his eye on the place."

"But we reckon you're up to it." Miloud sniggered. "And if the Feds catch you, you're under age. You'll be all right."

Samir looked away. His cousins were dumping him in it. He felt sick as he pushed the car door open, only to be grabbed roughly by the neck and pulled back. Rachid pinned him down and pressed the knife against his throat.

"Wait, we haven't finished yet, Samir. You're fond of your little sister, aren't you? So listen up. If you get caught, if they interrogate you, and if you give us away ... are you hearing me, Samir?"

"Yes," Samir breathed, half strangled by his jacket collar.

"You won't be seeing your sister again. We'll put an end to little Gem's suffering. Am I talking English proper now?"

Samir's cousins eventually let him go, bruised, shaking with anger, and several miles from Hummingbird Tower. He wasn't bothered about them threatening him. He wasn't interested in his own life. But they'd dragged his little sister into it. His only sister, who he affectionately called Lulu, but who his cousins called Gem. Gem as in GM: genetically modified.

Lulu was sick with a genetic disease.

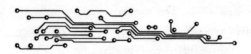

Aisha Lets On

Majid looked glumly at his New Generation BIT monitor with its handsome electric blue shell. Mrs Badach had covered it in a sort of plastic nightie and taped over the slots on the base unit. His computer meant much more to Majid than just a bound and gagged PC. It meant a space without walls where he could escape life on the estate. It meant Calimero and the strange game they should have kept a secret.

Suddenly Majid had an alarming thought. Calimero could still go on playing Golem. He could play without Magic Berber. Now that really *was* unfair. He'd have to stop him.

Hugh wished he could stop himself. Whenever Golem flashed up on the screen, he turned away as if to say, "Not interested." But the game found ways of harassing him, and some of them were quite weird. For example, a small white golem appeared on the screen, like a screen mate, moving up and down the margins or crossing on a diagonal, shaking its head apologetically. Hugh was sure he hadn't installed this program. But since he couldn't get rid of it, he resigned himself to the invasion. He even gave his new companion a name: Joke.

That evening, Hugh felt a strong urge to click on the game and set off in search of Natasha. He thought about her nostalgically, like a holiday romance. His hand hovered over the mouse. But the sound of the phone ringing drilled into his brain. Mrs Mullins appeared.

"What now?" Hugh spluttered, grabbing the receiver.

"Hello, sir?" said a shy voice on the other end.

It was Majid. Majid, not Magic Berber any more.

"Evening," said Hugh, a bit embarrassed.

There was an awkward silence, until Majid couldn't hold back any longer. "You're not playing by yourself, are you?"

Hugh felt like he'd been caught red-handed. "Of course not. Haven't gone near it!" he protested in a tone of voice Mamadou would have been proud of.

Silence again. Calimero made a spur of the moment decision. "Are you still barred from using your computer?"

"Yes."

"Why don't we try and strike some kind of deal with your mum?" Hugh lowered his voice so that his own mother wouldn't hear. "We'll tell her you're going to take your work seriously from now on. I could drop by and have a word with her, if you like. But I mean it. You'll have to knuckle down. You're a bright kid, Majid. I promise it'll only take two weeks to get your marks back on track…"

"Two weeks?" Majid groaned. "Yeah, right. More like two months, Calimero. And you get to play all that time."

Hugh smiled when he heard Majid using his

player's name. Magic Berber was back. "I won't, I promise," he insisted, not realizing how difficult it would be to keep his word.

It was on the tip of Majid's tongue to let Calimero know he had something important to tell him. But the words stuck in his throat. No, he and Aisha would keep their secrets.

First of all there was the white blobby thing that sparked in the dark basements. Majid couldn't make up his mind about it. Maybe it wasn't real at all. Then there was the smoke without fire that Aisha had seen coming from under the Badachs' front door. That sparked too. Just to convince themselves it had really happened, they ran their hands over the scorch mark along the door frame. They both got a bigger electric shock than Aisha had experienced the first time, as if the static was building up.

Majid couldn't explain it at all. But Aisha had ideas of her own. Her great-uncle was a witch doctor in Mali, and she'd heard about strange things happening back home. She believed in the souls of dead people coming back to haunt the living.

According to her, Hummingbird Tower was haunted by evil spirits from the basements all the way up to the twelfth floor. According to Majid, evil spirits only existed in horror films. Whenever they got a moment alone, they had long discussions about who was right.

Majid got a real shock when he walked into Mrs Cure's class one morning. Aisha, who usually stuck to Nouria like they were joined at the hip, was sitting next to Sebastian. Majid guessed she was trying to copy last night's algebra homework. But Aisha wasn't cheating. She was actually talking to Sebastian the geek. And, as if that wasn't amazing enough, Sebastian was talking back to her. Majid fumed as he tried to concentrate on those crazy letters 8D were meant to be adding up like numbers. Their tiny teacher was all fired up about them, but they didn't do it for him.

At break he wanted some answers. But Aisha and Sebastian took themselves off to a corner of the playground. Majid wasn't the only one who felt betrayed. Nouria was pulling a long face. She came over to Majid.

"Have you seen?" she asked, pointing to the other end of the playground. "Her and that geek!"

"They can talk if they like," muttered Majid.

"Oh yeah? D'you know what they're talking about? Ghosts!"

He flinched. "What d'you mean? What ghosts?"

"You ready for a shock? Well, get this – they're electric ghosts!" Nouria sneered.

Majid's jaw dropped. Aisha was telling the whole world his secret.

Ghosts... Majid thought he saw one that evening, as he was passing Big B Stores. The ghost of Aisha. There she was, standing by the supermarket exit, staring at her basket and looking dazed. He didn't know what to do. He wasn't the kind of boy to pick a fight with a girl, so he carried on. But Aisha looked up and saw him.

"Majid!"

She sounded upset. Against his better judgement, he headed over to her. What did he have to say to a girl who couldn't keep a secret?

"Majid..." Aisha was crying. "I lost the money when I was running here."

"You lost the money?"

"My dad's going to kill me."

Majid knew how strict her dad could be. He was still feeling bitter, but he asked a few questions all the same. "Where did you lose it? How much? What were you meant to buy?"

"Mighty B milkshake, a bottle of Big B cola and some sweet potatoes."

They set off side by side towards Hummingbird Tower, scouring the ground to see if the money had taken root somewhere. Majid could hear Aisha sobbing at each step, and he started giving himself a hard time. Maybe she hadn't let him down, after all. She'd only told Nouria, hadn't she? And wasn't that what best friends were for? They reached the concrete towers of the estate.

"If you like," he said reluctantly, "we could ask my mum for the money."

Aisha gave him a radiant smile. Everyone knew how kind-hearted Mrs Badach was. Quicker than a hummingbird, she planted a kiss on his cheek. He kept telling himself she'd never have mentioned anything to Sebastian. But the simplest thing was to ask her outright. They climbed the stairs together.

"You didn't tell Sebastian about the ghost, did you?"

Aisha blushed to the roots of her hair. "It's not my fault," she stammered. "I can't sleep in the dark any more. I turn the light on and my dad shouts because I'm wasting electricity."

"So it's true?" Majid asked crisply. "You let on."

"I'm scared of spirits. That's why I talked to Sebastian."

They'd reached the twelfth floor. Aisha looked imploringly at Majid. She was so pretty, with her sad soulful eyes. He felt a stab of jealousy.

"And you think spirits are scared of geeks?"

"It's not that."

"You think Sebastian knows how to get rid of ghosts?"

"No." Then, to Majid's surprise, she back-tracked. "Well, yes. Maybe."

It turned out that Sebastian wasn't just top of their class. He was also an expert on ghosts, vampires and werewolves. He had the complete *Nightmare on Elm Street* collection at home, together with every book ever written on the subjects of spiritualism, and white and black magic. If anybody could drive the evil spirits out of Hummingbird Tower, it was Sebastian the geek.

Grey Matter

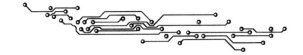

Hugh looked morosely at the plate next to his key-board. Cream crackers, a foil triangle of processed cheese and three pieces of ham. His supper. Some days, his mum just wasn't in the mood for cooking.

"You're bored, aren't you?" he said to the little warrior, who was sulking with his visor down and his arms folded.

Night had long since fallen over the Moreland Estate. But Golemia was bathed in bright sunshine. Why stay here? Why wait, when one simple click…? It was a reflex action. Hugh picked up the game again, or the game picked him up. His scowl turned into a smile.

"Hi, Natasha!"

There she was, in her room with its glowing hearth and four-poster bed. The advantage of virtual girls was you always knew where to find them.

"What d'you fancy, sweetheart? Go for a meal, chill in a club or get some sleep?"

Sophisticated as the game might be, Hugh still couldn't talk to the girl-golem directly. He had to press the space bar to activate the little warrior. He'd have preferred to conduct his relationship without this electronic third party. When the little warrior was in front of Natasha, a scroll unfurled with the following headings:

intelligence
character
special powers
skills

He clicked on the first line. The image zoomed in on Natasha's face, taking his breath away. Her shiny eyes and luscious lips were cover-girl material. But she was such an accurate copy, even her eyes were like those of glossy beauties. Blank.

"Where were you the day the brains got given out?" he wondered.

Calimero tried a few different keys. When he pressed ENTER, the girl-golem's room disappeared. For a moment he thought he'd been ejected from the game, but he'd just changed location.

In front of him, among the scary graphics of twisted trees and sinister ruins, was a skull on an expanse of red sand. If you looked through its eye sockets, you could see a palpitating green substance.

"I didn't realize grey matter was so green," he whispered.

He edged the little warrior forward. Close up, he saw the skull was castle-shaped. Instead of ears, it had crenellated turrets made of bone. Its rickety teeth looked like crumbling ramparts.

Calimero was on full alert, keeping an eye on the creepy-crawlies swarming all around. But the attack came from the skull itself. The gaping holes in its nose were like shadowy caves. Spurts of smoking liquid gushed out. The little warrior was hit. The next moment he turned bright red and started flashing alarmingly. He was losing life points.

"Keep calm..." Hugh muttered.

The retreating warrior kept fighting, shooting arrows right and left. Hugh sent Bubble into the front line. The dragon's fire worked wonders. In the space of a few seconds, the nostril ditches were wiped clean of their invisible occupants and the little warrior was...

"Back at the foot of the skull!" Hugh strained his neck to catch a glimpse of the top of the skull, way above his screen. He thought a moment and then tried c. Bull's-eye! It was the key that made the little warrior crawl, but it also granted him rock-climbing talents. The warrior reached the edge of the right eye socket and leant against it.

"Now what?"

The game answered Hugh with its old type-writer rattle:

Choose your weapon, Calimero!

He hit a key at random. q nearly proved fatal. The little warrior made a dangerous leap on the narrow rim. Hugh watched him flap his arms before miraculously regaining his balance.

Try harder, Calimero!

"The numbers!" Hugh shouted, hitting his forehead.

The numbers gave him access to the weapons. He already knew about 1 and 6. He tried 4 and was given an enormous pea-shooter.

"Bingo! But what am I meant to do with it?" he wondered.

He pressed ENTER without holding out much hope. The pea-shooter began to tilt upright in the warrior's hands, until it came into contact with the green substance. At the same time, Natasha's sweet face appeared at an angle to the screen. A dotted line stretched under her chin:

0 _ 200

Hugh pressed ENTER again. This was followed by a revolting sucking sound. The little warrior was sipping the giant brain, using the pea-shooter as his straw.

"Hic!"

Each time he pressed a key, one of the dashes lit up, and, since he didn't know what else to do, he started counting them. "Five, six..." He was taken aback. "Am I imagining things?"

Natasha's face looked different. Or maybe it was just her eyes.

"Eighteen, nineteen…" He burst out laughing. He'd got it now. The dashes that lit up showed how clever Natasha was. In other words, her IQ.

"An IQ of eighty, darling. Not exactly a rocket scientist. Let's give you ten more. That's more like it. You're starting to look like an 8D now."

Her face was slowly looking brighter. Hugh's new powers had gone to his head, and he just kept on pressing.

0 _ 200

"Yeah! One hundred and eighty!"

But what he saw in the girl-golem's pupils made him shudder. Her expression was almost diabolical.

"Being too clever is bad for you. Anyway, how's that going to make me look? And it's no good if I can't understand you."

What was his own IQ? Hugh allotted himself a modest one hundred and forty. But how could he get Natasha's down again? He pressed ESC and was relieved to see that the luminous dashes were disappearing: one hundred and seventy, one hundred and sixty... *Schlurp!* The spewed-out brains made an obscene noise. The system froze at one hundred and fifty. Then the image misted over, as if an invisible hand was mixing lots of colours to give the screen a new coat of paint.

An hour later, Hugh still couldn't work out whether he'd heard somebody laughing when the game crashed.

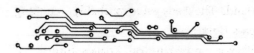

Behind Door 401

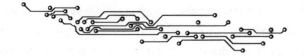

Samir's parents had been arguing again. For a change. They'd stormed out of the flat leaving Lulu's big brother to look after her. For a change. It was bad timing. Even worse than usual.

Luckily, Lulu was asleep. Samir gazed at her tiny body curled up in a bed three times too big for her, and the anger welled up inside him. He remembered how his cousins had talked about her.

"They're just cowards," he explained to his sleeping sister. "They make all these plans, and then..."

Then they get Samir to carry them out.

"It sucks."

It was his own fault. What a stupid idea to try

and trap Majid. The Feds were probably watching the basements right now.

"I've left your medicine on Koala's tummy. If you wake up…"

Lulu whimpered in her sleep. What if I go to prison? Samir wondered. Who'll think about Lulu's medicine then? She might die. He felt a rush of pride at the idea that his sister's survival depended on him. He closed the door gently and headed down to the basements.

The timer-switch was on the blink again. But Samir had come prepared. He had a huge torch to light his way and a strap to tie it around his neck. That way his hands were free.

The basements were his cousins' area. Or their crew's, at any rate. Raves, secret meetings, hide-outs. Nobody outside their tribe dared set foot there any more.

The large wooden door creaked loudly enough to wake up all of Hummingbird Tower. Samir stood there, heart thumping, and counted to ten. Then he headed down, a big beam of light ahead of him.

"311, 312…"

Counting out loud helped calm his nerves. The numbers were clumsily marked in white and the paint had run. Most of the doors were smashed in. Behind them he could see the rubbish people had dumped there. Boxes, broken glass, piles of old clothes, empty bottles… Thousands of empty bottles.

He knew what came after a sharp bend in the corridor. The ghost.

"Hi, Prosper, how's it going?"

The ghost was holding the folds of its white shroud delicately between its finger bones. Its mouth was a hole and its eyes were blank, but there was nothing to be scared of. Since the day a graffiti artist had scrawled him on one of the basement walls, nobody had ever seen Prosper move. Or almost nobody.

Why me?

Suddenly he was horrified to feel a hand stroking his hair. He turned round sharply. Prosper, who hadn't moved an inch, was acting innocent. Samir felt sick as he ran his fingers through his hair. "Grimy!" He'd just noticed the grey threads caught in the beam from his torch. Everybody knew that

spiders and ghosts were friends. Like rats. Like...
No, he wasn't going to go there. Just follow the
corridor and count the doors. Lot 401, Miloud had
said.

Samir walked down a few slippery steps. The
deeper he went, the hotter it got. The hotter it got,
the more the walls glistened with damp. Weird. If
he hung around too long, he'd end up rotting.

He heard a noise.

"Who's there?"

No answer. He forced a laugh. Just the sound of
his own footsteps. He'd never gone as far as 401
before. He'd never gone further than the enormous
boiler that made creepy sighing noises every thirty
seconds. He went past two reinforced metal doors
that were padlocked. No numbers on them.

Suddenly he stopped in his tracks and listened.

"That's not me!"

Samir hadn't moved. So it couldn't be the sound
of his own footsteps. Must be Prosper stretching his
legs. Or the boiler clearing its pipes. Yes, that was
it, the boiler.

Lot 401. There it was. A collapsed worm-eaten
door. But the number was clear to see.

Samir edged forward behind the broad shaft of light coming from his chest. He passed a load of bottles that looked like bristles sticking out of a pile of cast-iron hedgehogs. Then he got tangled up in a bundle of old sheets. Finally he skirted round a coal heap.

Bits of broken glass made a nasty crunching noise underfoot. He felt the darkness closing in on him.

"Not now! Don't pack up now!" he begged, tapping his torch.

But it was still working. It was just that this lot was so enormous.

Before dropping him off, Miloud and Rachid had given Samir detailed instructions.

"You go past the coal, Samir. You'll see a dead rat after that. It stops people being too nosy. Step over the rolls of barbed wire. And when you reach the wall, there's a sort of alcove. A hole, you get us? Pull out the rags. Take the box. And remember. Respect. We're talking two grand's worth of gear, Samir."

Everything was going to plan. Well, almost. The

dead rat had gone. Samir would've preferred it to be there. He wanted things to be just the way his cousins had described them.

The box was heavy. Shallow but heavy. All he had to do was make sure he wasn't caught now. But there was a problem. When he held the box, it blocked the torch. The trapped light made his stomach look red but it barely lit his surroundings. His feet got tangled in the barbed wire, his ankles got badly scratched and he nearly went flying.

He wondered about wearing the box on his head. I'll carry it the way women do in Senegal. If Mamadou could see me now! He managed five steps, but the box was too heavy, too big, too unbalanced. He couldn't fit it under his arm. He held it to his chest again and started shuffling forward, feeling in the gloom with his feet. Old clothes, broken glass.

All of a sudden he started seeing much better, even though the torch was useless. Somebody must have got the timer-switch working. They'd be waiting for him up there. He'd get caught. Then he spotted a light bulb. Not a glimmer. So it wasn't coming from that. It was coming from…

That thing.

It wasn't a man. Or a mountain. It was a monster. Samir clutched the box, as if nothing in the world mattered more than keeping it safe. The creature was blocking his path, between the hedgehogs with bottle haircuts and the door of 401. Samir was convinced it was going to eat him, but it wasn't in a hurry.

He took the opportunity to get a good look. It was enormous and throbbing. At least, he guessed it was... The more he looked, the less he knew what it looked like. It didn't have a definite shape. It was a cross between Mr Clean and Frankenstein's monster. It was whiter than Prosper and brighter than his B Power torch. Its head was the scariest part. It looked keen and sad and expressionless, all at the same time.

And it looked dead.

Samir didn't want to be eaten alive without putting up a fight. If there'd just been him to think about, he'd probably have given up. But what about Lulu?

He lost his grip on the box and it landed on his foot. He felt a sharp stab of pain, but that was the least of his worries. The monster had reacted to being struck by the light from his torch. Its whole body started flashing blue sparks, like the ones you see at the top of dodgem poles. Samir thought he knew what that crackling sound meant. The creature wasn't going to eat him raw. It was going to fry him first.

And soon. Because it was heading straight for him.

He crouched down and started to grope about on the floor, without taking his eyes off the monster. He needed a weapon, something to throw. Could you frighten it? Could you hurt it? What if it ate glass and metal? Coal. Where was the pile of coal? He remembered that the name for those small black lumps was nuts. He'd pelt the creature with nuts.

Finally his scrabbling left hand found something. It was soft and damp. Out of the corner of his eye he saw what he'd picked up. The rat. The dead rat. He gasped in horror and hurled the rodent with all his strength towards the creature. A big flash of light followed, and the rat vanished into thin air.

"Holy Mecca!"

A wave of terror swept over him. Run. Run for your life. He tried to get to his feet. But something was pulling him back, strangling him. His legs skidded on the damp floor. He panicked. He was suffocating, pinned down like a prisoner in the dust. The torch strap! It had got caught. That was what was strangling him.

Samir tugged at the strap, but the creature was already bearing down on him, drowning him in its ghastly brightness. He tried to free himself again, but the strap was cutting into his neck. He couldn't breathe. He was going to die.

He didn't want to die. He was fumbling desperately now. The strap had snagged on the barbed wire. He could feel the spikes gashing his fingers, ripping the palms of his hands. Come on, one clean tug. *One more.*

Samir fell backwards, half knocking himself out on a large glass bottle. He was free. But it was too late. As the hideous white creature leant over him, blue sparks flashing all around, he was sorry he hadn't been strangled by his own torch strap. Sorry he wasn't dead.

At 11.30 p.m. the caretaker of Hummingbird Tower took Brutus out for the second time that evening. It was one of those nights when the dog was nervous and edgy. The caretaker had a smoke while Brutus sprayed a bollard.

On his way back, the caretaker was surprised to see a ray of light seeping under the door leading to the basements. Was somebody in there? But the timer-switch hadn't been working for three days now. Brutus started growling and bared his teeth. He was drooling.

There was a disturbing noise, a sort of small explosion, and everything went dark again. The caretaker listened for a bit and then decided to pretend he hadn't noticed. At sixty, he reckoned he'd still got plenty of years left in him for beer and bingo. Why take unnecessary risks for the sake of a few old planks of wood and a pile of broken bottles?

He could wait till the morning to see if the lights had mysteriously come back on again.

At 11.30 p.m., by a strange coincidence, Aisha was as edgy as Brutus. An urgent call of nature woke her. She wanted to forget about it and go back to sleep, but it was no use. She got up reluctantly, throwing the end of her sheet over her bedside lamp. Reassured by its glow, she made her way down the corridor towards the toilet. It was dark. Apart from under the front door. She could make out a painful glare on the other side. The electric smoke!

She ran all the way back to bed and tucked herself up again, legs clenched, heart pounding. Her eyes were glued to the bedroom door. *Ping!* Her light bulb went *phut*.

At 11.30 p.m. Mr Badach had just come in. Slumped in his armchair, he was watching TV with a plate of cold meat on his knees. He'd turned the sound right down so as not to wake his family. All of a sudden the picture went blurry. Then the programme disappeared altogether. He was left with a snowy screen and a shadow, which seemed to come from somewhere else, moving backwards and forwards across it.

At 11.30 p.m. Hugh was in front of his computer. He was hard at it, for a change.

"Push off! I've got work to do," he told the little white golem.

But Joke wanted to play. He'd come looking for Hugh, like a dog bringing its ball back.

"Not tonight. Clear off!"

He frowned. For the first time, Joke had frozen in the middle of the screen and was deliberately blocking Hugh's document while shaking his head. And, for the first time, Hugh thought there was something threatening about Joke.

Meanwhile, deep in the basements of Hummingbird Tower, on the other side of door 401, a child was bellowing in the dark.

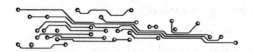

Two Shrinkers Plus One

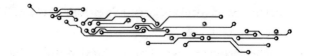

The Shrinkers had shrunk to two. When Mrs Badach opened her front door in the middle of the afternoon, she was surprised to find them on the landing.

"Sorry to trouble you," said the first one, who was tall and skinny, with a face like a knife.

"We're from Price Shrinkers," said the second, who was young but had totally white hair. Mrs Badach thought he looked unhealthy because of his pasty face, and dangerous because of his boxer's nose.

"Ah! You bring photo!" she guessed, remembering how she'd posed as a happy winner beside the handsome computer for the next catalogue.

The two men gave each other a confused look.

"Photo? What photo?" asked the skinny bloke.

Mrs Badach was shocked by the way they barged into the flat. There were so many stories about dodgy characters taking advantage of housewives. Luckily, Majid finished school at four o'clock. He wouldn't be long.

The intruders were trying to be friendly, but it was clearly an effort. And Mrs Badach didn't like the way they were examining her living room. As if they were looking for things to steal.

"It's because of the computer," said Shrinker No. 1.

"There's been a mistake," added Shrinker No. 2.

"We've very sorry."

"We've brought another one with us."

"It's on the landing."

The way they took it in turns, you'd think they'd learnt their lines off by heart.

"Other komputer? What story you iz telling me?"

"Haven't you been having some problems with your machine?" asked the one whose face was as white as chalk.

Mrs Badach stood there for a moment, confused. How did they know about it? "Well, yes. My son, he no work at skool, innit."

"We're talking about disturbances," Chalk Face explained. "Incidents. Breakdowns."

"Aaaah!" This time Mrs Badach understood. So she told them. About the kettle that kept going on the blink. The plugs that kept fusing. Only last night her husband had seen strange things on the TV.

The two men nodded.

"It's just as we thought," Skinny Bloke declared. "The machine we delivered was faulty. You mustn't use it any more."

"Iz no chance. Majid he iz punished."

"We're going to do an exchange," said Chalk Face. "The one you've got here is dangerous. A dud. It happens sometimes."

Mrs Badach wasn't sure about this. They hadn't won her confidence, these Shrinkers. And anyway, why were there only two of them? Weren't there supposed to be three? It was hard always being alone, without a man around the place.

Mrs Badach was right. There *was* a third Shrinker. Right now he was getting out of the khaki-coloured four-wheel drive parked in front of Hummingbird Tower.

This could take some time, he reckoned, lighting a cigarette. People were so suspicious these days. They'd need convincing before agreeing to the swap. And then, to make it seem more legit, his colleagues would have to install the new computer. Show them it worked. Point out how sleek and fast it was…

Huh – he'd done the right thing staying down here. To pass the time he got out his mobile phone and tried calling his girlfriend. But the sexy voice on the other end belonged to the answerphone. So he found another way of passing the time.

His handset wasn't on the market yet. A state-of-the-art New Generation BIT phone. He pressed a few buttons and picked up the game of battleships he'd left off at lunchtime. Riveting.

Up on the twelfth floor, Mrs Badach was protesting. "No, stop!"

But the two men weren't taking no for an

answer. They'd pushed several big cardboard boxes into the living room and were cutting through the packing tape with a Stanley knife.

"You won't say that when you've seen it," Chalk Face assured her.

The harder they tried to convince her, the more suspicious Mrs Badach became. Nobody begs you to accept a good deal. Life had taught her that. Something she'd heard her children say kept going round in her head: you can't take a present back, or it's stealing. So she threw herself onto the biggest box, at the risk of getting mutilated by the Stanley knife.

"No, wait for Majid," she implored. "Wait for Majid."

"Your son won't believe his luck, lady."

"Be a nice surprise for him."

The two men were making a supreme effort to be calm and polite. But the looks they kept giving each other betrayed their irritation. Mrs Badach was relieved when she heard the key turning in the lock.

"Emmay, hayé— Who are they?"

Emmay spoke in Berber to put Majid in the picture as rapidly as possible. The Shrinkers didn't look very happy about this.

"When you've finished muttering your hocus-pocuses," said Chalk Face.

"Yeah, what kind of mumbo-jumbo d'you call that?" asked Skinny Bloke.

They tried separating Majid from his mother, so they could have a word with him on the side.

"Now listen, kid ... Majid ... that's your name, isn't it?" Chalk Face started. "Inside this box there's the most powerful processor on the market, a CD-writer—"

"Handy that, a good CD-writer, if you want to make yourself a bit of pocket money," his colleague hinted.

"—twenty-five free software applications and a top of the range ink-jet colour printer."

Majid was wavering. A printer was just what he needed. As for the CD-writer ... he knew boys at school who made nuff dollars running off bulk copies of the latest CDs and computer games.

But he was as suspicious as he was keen.

"Made your mind up, kid?"

He didn't like the man's tone of voice. He didn't like it at all.

Sunk! Down at the bottom of the building, Shrinker No. 3 had just lost a cruiser. He was ready to launch a counter-attack, but something kept interrupting his game.

A shape had been lurking on his mobile screen for the last two minutes. It kept clouding the game, coming and going, then disappearing altogether. Shrinker No. 3 noticed the fuzzy reception was linked to the angle of the aerial. Soon, he was more interested in this than his game of battleships. He noticed the shape became clearer each time he pointed the aerial towards the main entrance of Hummingbird Tower.

Interesting. Very interesting.

There was a man standing in the entrance hall, a bag of tools in his hand. It was the caretaker, and he'd just put in new fuses for the basement lights. Shrinker No. 3 waited for him to head off with his dog.

Right, the coast was clear … and… Blimey, the thing on the screen had a head – a head that looked vaguely familiar. What was going on?

Shrinker No. 3 made his way into Hummingbird Tower, brandishing the mobile like a magic wand. Suddenly the phone started crackling and sparking. Was that the lift door over there, on the left? No, it must be the way to the basements. Shrinker No. 3 wondered if this was a good idea. But he couldn't help it. He felt the pull of something stronger than him. The door was unlocked. He went in and pressed the timer-switch. The bulbs glowed brightly, dimmed, faltered ... and then cut out.

In his right-hand jacket pocket he had a pencil torch. Delivery men are always well equipped. Fact.

Another fact. Just because somebody says they're from Price Shrinkers, it doesn't mean they are.

Up on the twelfth floor, Emmay had taken refuge in a corner of the living room. She'd folded her arms and wasn't budging. Distraught, she watched her son putting up a fight against the two men, whose behaviour had suddenly become much more aggressive.

"Don't touch that!" Majid shouted when Chalk Face started disconnecting the monitor on the dining table.

"OK, that's enough now!" said Skinny Bloke, losing his temper. "We've told you, that machine's dangerous! D'you want to blow up the whole building?"

Majid clung to the base unit. He was thinking about what was inside it, about the game. They wanted to stop him playing Golem, he was sure of that. He had to warn Calimero. He was the only one who—

Chalk Face lifted him off the ground and set him back down again a bit further off. "Listen, kid. We've been nice enough so far. But if you don't get it, then tough. We'll take the whole lot away and send you a Game Boy, OK?"

"Emmay!" Majid called out. "Call Calim— Call Hugh. The teacher, Emmay, the teacher!"

Mrs Badach was so paralysed with emotion she couldn't move a finger. By a strange coincidence, a phone rang.

Chalk Face let go of Majid. He recognized his mobile's ring. Furiously he pulled it out of his pocket.

"Yeah? What?" he barked like a Rottweiler. "Sven?"

"He should've come up," muttered Skinny Bloke. "This is getting out of hand…"

His associate was signalling to him to shut up.

"Where are you? Answer me! Sven? Sven?"

The mobile made an eerie crackling noise loud enough for everybody in the room to hear. Then it went dead.

"Sven? Sven?"

Chalk Face shook the mobile like it was a rattle.

"What's he up to now?" asked Skinny Bloke.

Chalk Face could hardly turn any paler. But Mrs Badach and Majid could see from his expression how bewildered he was.

"Something's happened," he said. "We'd better go and see."

"Where?"

Chalk Face shrugged. "That's what I want to find out." He looked angrily around him. Majid had gone back to his computer. His arms were crossed and he was baring his teeth like a puppy.

"Come on!" urged Skinny Bloke.

The two men lifted the boxes they'd brought with them and exited, without shutting the door behind them.

"And that?" asked Emmay.

"What?"

Mrs Badach pointed to the parcel left behind in the hall. Majid bent over to get a better look. "It's the printer! They forgot the printer!"

Skinny Bloke and Chalk Face criss-crossed the Moreland Estate for over an hour in their four-wheel drive. Then, completely baffled, they called off the search.

What had happened to Sven?

A Visit to the Geek

Sebastian's parents had gone to the 8 p.m. screening at the Majestic Cinema, to watch a schmaltzy film. As far as Sebastian was concerned, a film without creaking doors and spurting blood was a waste of celluloid. Might as well stay at home and revise your science homework. At least you could project gory dissection scenes onto the screen of your imagination.

The sound of the doorbell startled him. Who could it be? It was too late for door-to-door salesmen flogging vacuum cleaners, and too early for the living dead.

"Well, I never… Hello."

"Hi," said Samir.

Sebastian stared at his classmate in surprise.

"Can I come in?"

"You weren't at school today."

"Wasn't in the mood."

Samir looked intimidated as he shuffled in. In the hall light, Sebastian noticed a bruise on his forehead and black marks on his neck. Then he saw that his left arm was bandaged from his elbow to his wrist. He also had an impressive collection of plasters on his fingers.

"You auditioning for a part in *The Mummy Returns Again and Again*?"

"Sebastian, I've got to talk to you."

"You mean you actually know my name?"

They'd been in the same class for two years, but Samir had always called Sebastian a geek. With a few variations. Fat geek. Or stupid geek. Samir didn't vary his variations much.

"Why don't you come up to my room?" Sebastian suggested. "My parents are out. They're at the Majestic."

"Mine are at the Moreland Arms."

Samir obviously thought the Majestic was a pub.

Sebastian didn't bother setting him straight.

Samir stopped in his tracks in front of Sebastian's library. Shelves and shelves of carefully arranged books. Black covers, red covers, gold covers...

"You're not telling me you've read all this stuff?"

"I've read some of them seven times. Like *The Secret of the Pyramids* and *The Wizards Are Among Us*."

"What's the point?"

Sebastian didn't have an answer to that, so he changed the subject. "What happened? Did somebody beat you up?"

"Perhaps you could say that." Samir carried on examining the books, craning his injured neck to try and read the titles. "*Life After Death*," he reeled off, "*Haunted Towers*."

"Are you looking for something?"

Samir put a finger on *Ghosts, Ghouls and the Living Dead*, only to pull it back quickly as if he'd got burnt. "Where do ghosts live?"

"Everybody knows that," Sebastian sneered. After two years of being treated like dirt, he wondered if sweet revenge was coming his way at last.

"Where then?"

"In castles, of course. Or manor houses. You know, really old places with bloodstains on the tiles that won't come off, no matter how hard you scrub them."

"Why blood?" Samir was clutching his left arm awkwardly.

"Because somebody got murdered a long time ago." Remembering something he'd read in a book supported by lots of documentary evidence, Sebastian quoted: "'We mustn't forget that the ghost is first and foremost a victim.'"

Samir was lost in thought for a moment. "D'you really believe that rubbish?"

"According to certain world experts—"

"Yeah, all right. Forget it. What about on the Moreland Estate?"

"What d'you mean, on the Moreland Estate?"

"Are there any? I mean, any ghosts there?"

Sebastian burst out laughing. "Maybe in a thousand years, when you come back to haunt the scene of your crimes."

Samir wasn't amused. "In Hummingbird Tower," he whispered.

"What?"

All of a sudden Samir started shouting. "I'm telling you, there's a ghost in Hummingbird Tower! A monster! A crazy thing! It nearly…"

Sebastian was astonished to see Samir's face screwed up with emotion. Even more surprising, tears were rolling down his cheeks. Loud-mouth Samir, rude-boy Samir, was sobbing like a big girl's blouse.

Sebastian didn't know what to do, so he made him sit down on the bed. "D'you want something to drink?"

"I'm done for," Samir groaned.

"No, you're not. Come on." Sebastian tried to reason with him. "You're safe here."

"I can't do it! I can't go back there! It drank something. And now it's even stronger."

"You sure you're not the one who drank something?"

Samir shook his head. "I saw it."

"Who…" Sebastian asked patiently, as if he was talking to an invalid, "…drank *what*?"

"The monster. It drank the light. The B Power torch."

Sebastian had read at least three hundred books about the paranormal, aliens and creatures from outer space. He never missed an episode of *The X-Files* or a TV documentary about the super-natural. But this was the first time he'd heard of a monster drinking B Power torches.

"They're gonna kill me," Samir spluttered.

"You mean there's lots of them?"

"Not it, you plonk— Sebastian. My cousins!"

"Your cousins are monsters?" Not many people on the Moreland Estate would have argued with that.

"Their gear's still down there."

Sebastian took a deep breath and tried to focus his mind. "I'm going to get you a Big B cola," he offered. "And then you're going to tell me all about it, from the beginning. Because right now you've lost me."

Samir gave Sebastian a detailed account of his journey to hell, starting with his cousins' threat and lot 401, followed by the appearance of the creature and the fight.

"It was right on top of me. I thought it was

going to eat me, electrocute me…" Samir gulped down some Big B cola. "But all it did was swallow the torch." He broke off. His hand was shaking so much, the cola was making waves inside his glass.

"So it wasn't the monster who did all this to you?" asked Sebastian, nodding at Samir's collection of plasters and bandages.

"I got tangled up in the barbed wire lying around, and then there was all the rest of the rubbish. I ran. I couldn't see. I kept bumping into things. I don't know how I got out."

"There's definitely some weird stuff going on at the moment," Sebastian announced. "The other day, Aisha told me she keeps seeing strange smoke on the twelfth floor of Hummingbird Tower." He thought for a moment, before adding, "Maybe a graveyard…"

"You what?"

"I can't see what else it'd be," he said, warming to the idea. "You don't usually get paranormal phenomena in a modern tower block. So we need an explanation. If you ask me, the tower was built on top of an old graveyard. They're trying to get out."

"Who?"

"The dead people."

Samir looked amazed as he digested this. "You think I met a dead person?"

"Probably a condemned soul."

The cola leapt inside Samir's glass. "And do your books mention condemned souls eating B Power torches?"

"I've never heard of it before," Sebastian had to admit. "The thing is, I haven't actually read *all* of them."

"You've got to help me."

Sebastian felt his chest puffing up with pride. In his wildest dreams, he'd never imagined Samir begging him like this. But why was his head throbbing? And what was that queasy feeling in his stomach? It felt suspiciously like fear.

"You don't want to go to the police?" he asked in a quavering voice. Sebastian knew the Feds wouldn't swallow a story like that. They weren't trained in the supernatural. Which was why so many mysterious cases remained unsolved.

"You're forgetting about the gear," Samir reminded him.

Sebastian was beginning to understand why

Samir was still green with terror. Even when he was safe and sound, sipping his cola.

There are three possibilities, he thought. One, Samir goes back to get the gear and is gobbled up by the ghost of Hummingbird Tower. Two, he doesn't get the gear and is killed by his cousins. Three, he tells the police everything.

But there was a fourth option. According to Samir.

"You've got to be joking!" Sebastian shouted. "You want me to put my life on the line for you?" He noticed Samir's eyes light up with a sinister hope.

"You're the expert. You must have stuff against condemned souls."

"Stuff?"

"I don't know – magic potions, wizards' gizmos. Stuff, get it?"

"I'd have to do some research first," Sebastian said cautiously.

Samir switched tack. "So what's the point of reading all these books? You're just a geek. That's what I've always said. A geek and a loser."

"I haven't said no yet."

The more Sebastian thought about it, the more he was inclined to agree with Samir. What *was* the point of spending all those years reading so many books and watching so many films, if he wasn't ready for the big moment when it came? Here was Samir offering him the case of a lifetime, and offering it on a plate. If he turned it down, he really *was* a geek.

But he still had one lingering doubt. What if the whole thing was a bad joke?

"Not on my own, though," he declared. "If I do it, you're coming with me. And you're going first."

English Lessons

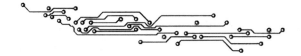

Take one person out of the equation and things start looking up, Hugh reflected.

Teaching 8D without Samir was a joy. All he had to do was keep an eye on Mamadou, confiscate Miguel's farting goo and stop Farida talking. He was also pleasantly surprised when he came to mark 8D's dictations. Majid had only made eleven mistakes, his best result since January.

Once he'd got the boring stuff over with, Hugh settled down in front of his computer. The game popped up without any prompting. A snatch of violin music was followed by a booming voice.

"Golemmmm."

Calimero was impatient to see his beloved again.

"Bust: thirty-eight. IQ: one hundred and fifty," he said dreamily. "You had a narrow escape there, darling. Imagine if it'd been the other way round!"

But Natasha wasn't complete yet. She needed special powers and skills, as well as a few weaknesses to spice her up.

Hugh had just given Natasha irresistible powers of seduction, when the phone rang in the sitting room.

"What mark did I get?"

"Majid?"

"What did you give me for the dictation?" Majid asked urgently. "I've got to pass."

"Eleven mistakes," Hugh told him. "Ten is a pass. But they weren't all serious ones."

"You put in words that don't even exist!" whined Majid. "Please. My mum promised."

"Promised what?"

"The computer. If I get a pass."

"She's too nice, your mum. That's her problem."

"I'm only allowed to use it for school work."

Hugh smiled. He'd make sure Majid got a good pass.

"Guess what?" Majid said suddenly. "I've got a printer!"

"Where from?" Hugh was alarmed now.

"It's all right, I swear. It's not like..." Majid didn't finish. He hadn't stolen it. But Hugh would never believe him if he just said somebody had "left" it round at his place.

"The Price Shrinkers came back," he explained.

Hugh was very interested in the story of the two delivery men. He found it hard to believe they were acting on the instructions of a mail-order firm. So whose orders *were* they following? And what did they want? Were they really interested in Majid's computer just because it was faulty?

Inevitably the conversation turned to Golem.

"Have you played it again?" Majid asked.

"A bit," Hugh stalled.

"Where've you got to?"

So, for the first time, Hugh described his girl-golem. Unwisely, he waxed lyrical about her charms. Majid brought him back down to earth with a bump.

"Are you in love or something?"

"It's … it's just a game," stammered Calimero, taken aback.

"Yeah, but wouldn't you like to know her in real life?"

Hugh gave an embarrassed laugh.

"What kind of special powers have you given her?"

"Well, I've only just started. But I was thinking of … er … seduction."

"That's not a special power!" Majid scoffed. "I'm going to make a real hero. And he'll be so fit, Natasha'll fall in love with him and you won't stand a chance—"

"Impossible," Hugh butted in. "I'm going to make Natasha discerning."

"Wassat?"

"It means she'll have good taste. Natasha will only like suave, sophisticated young English teachers."

This was greeted with peals of laughter.

"OK, goodnight, Magic Berber!"

"No, wait a second! What about my keyboard? You promised me a keyboard!"

Hugh agreed to get hold of one, and hung up.

He tried to behave like an adult and stop thinking about Joke and Natasha, but he couldn't get what Majid had told him about the Price Shrinkers out of his mind.

Playing the game was still out of the question back at the Badachs'. Majid plugged in his new keyboard, which he'd been given that morning after English. He switched on the computer and turned round. Emmay was lying peacefully on the sofa with her arms folded.

"You're not staying there, are you?" he grumbled.

Emmay nodded. "You do your work, Majid. Komputer iz for skool."

Majid had tasted a moment of pure happiness when he'd pressed the *on* button. But his mum's stubbornness was spoiling it.

"Not all the time?" he groaned.

"I know how what you iz like, Majid."

Emmay didn't trust him. She'd decided to watch over his shoulder whenever the machine was switched on. So there was no chance of wandering off to Golem City.

He typed a string of swear words on his new keyboard. "It's not like you can check on me. You don't even know how to read."

Tentatively Emmay leant forward and put a finger on the screen. "Go on. You tell them to me."

"Er … no," he said, quickly deleting everything he'd just written. "Hey, look at this!"

Emmay, he wrote.

"Iz my name," she said, sounding offended. "I know that!"

So Majid wrote Majid. Then he typed the names of Mrs Badach's six other sons: Abdelkarim, Monir, Omar, Haziz, Moussa, Brahim.

"I know, I know … iz my childrin. Show to me something else."

"Well, for a start," he said, "you don't say *iz my childrin*. You say *they are my children*. There!" And he wrote they are. "They are, they are," he repeated.

Feeling inspired, Majid added Hummingbird Tower, Aisha, couscous, Calimero, hello, thank you, dictation…

Lastly he typed: I love you, Emmay, and his mum started crying.

At school, lessons were all a bit of a blur. Miguel pummelled his farting goo and Mamadou practised weightlifting with his textbooks. Nothing had changed, except for one detail: Sebastian's seat in the front row was empty.

"Sit down! Sit down!" Hugh kept saying.

"Sit down!" bellowed Mamadou.

Immediately there was the deafening noise of bums on seats.

"Thanks for that, Mamadou. Right, where did we get to?"

"*Year 8 English, Texts and Approaches: The Greatest Hits Ever*," announced Nouria. "Page twenty-seven."

"Zeinul, would you volunteer to read out loud?"

There was a rustling of papers on Zeinul's desk. "Ready, sir. Do I start, like, now?" He cleared his throat and started reading: "'*Ow! Squelch! Whisssper! Miaow!*'"

"Excellent!" said Hugh. "Our lesson today is about words that are examples of onomatopoeia. So, their sound copies their meaning…"

Hugh was unnerved by Sebastian's absence. He felt disorientated without him. There was something encouraging about having that concentrated expression right under his nose, in the front row. Suddenly he saw him. Hidden away at the back of the class, next to Samir. Now where had *he* suddenly sprung from? Samir was putting in an appearance after being away for a few days, and he was covered in bruises and plasters.

Samir and Sebastian. An unlikely duo, thought Hugh, as 8D made an uncharacteristically enthusiastic contribution to the day's lesson.

"*Mii-aa-oo-ww!*"

"*W-oo-oo-ff-ff!*"

"*Sppp-la-ttt!*"

Hugh moved away from his desk, walked past Majid, who was doodling golems, and stood behind Samir and Sebastian. "Would you mind telling me what you're doing?"

The two boys were inspecting the contents of a Big B Stores plastic bag under the table. What was inside it? Pirated CDs? Hugh seized the bag and poked his nose inside.

"What on earth...?" To his astonishment, he pulled out a plait of garlic. "Canteen food not tasty enough?"

"It's for my mum's lamb casserole, sir."

Sebastian's excuse was so lame, it didn't even raise a titter from 8D.

"Great!" said Hugh. "Well, since you're in a mood for acting, let's do a spot of role-play. Samir, you can be Mr Bean after a DIY session. You look like him with all those plasters. Sebastian, you can be the chef at the restaurant he goes into, since you seem to have the right ingredients for the role. Zeinul, I'm counting on you to make the sound effects using onomatopoeic words."

"And me, sir?"

"And me, sir?"

"All right," said Hugh, giving in, "everybody can do the onomatopoeic words."

"RA-AA-AH!" went the class, roaring the best onomatopoeic word of all.

At break, they finalized their plans.

"You set for tomorrow evening?" asked Samir.

"I … I think so," Sebastian stammered.

"My cousins are getting itchy feet."

The two boys were thoughtful for a moment.

"I hope it's not a werewolf," said Sebastian after a while.

"And if it is?"

"We'll be in trouble. Garlic's for vampires. And I'm not stealing my mum's jewellery."

Samir looked blank.

"You can kill werewolves with silver bullets," Sebastian explained.

"Your mum's got weird taste in jewellery."

"You melt the jewellery down, idiot. And then you make it into bullets."

All of a sudden Samir felt depressed. His cousins were no nearer to getting their gear back. Luckily for him, whatever was haunting the basements didn't look like a werewolf.

Not one little bit.

Back to the Basements

The caretaker of Hummingbird Tower hadn't enjoyed taking Brutus out after dark the last few nights. There seemed to be a curse hanging over the tower block. A series of power failures, strange noises…

He was convinced there was something suspicious going on in the basements. If he'd been brave enough, he'd have hidden somewhere and kept a lookout. Over there, for instance, behind the big green dustbins. But watching Brutus put him off. That dog could make mincemeat of anybody, but now he was standing with his hackles up and his eyes rolling. And as for the way he was growling…

The caretaker cut short his walk, heading back as soon as Brutus had sprayed his favourite bollard.

"It's OK," whispered Sebastian. "He's going in now."

Samir was crouching next to him, hidden by an enormous delivery truck tyre. Sebastian looked up at the sky. It was garishly bright. A big fat reddish moon was floating just above Hummingbird Tower.

"I don't like it," he muttered.

"What?"

"The full moon," Sebastian said in a spooky voice. "I really hope we're not dealing with a werewolf." He'd packed everything he needed to confront the underground beast into his blue sports bag. But he was still missing the silver bullets essential for slaying werewolves.

Brutus and the caretaker had gone. Everything was calm on the estate. As he went into the tower block, Sebastian glanced up at the moon and wondered if he'd ever see it again.

"Careful with your torch," Samir reminded him, switching his own on.

They'd each got a torch, and they'd agreed that if the creature showed up, they'd hide them immediately. According to Samir, the monster was like a moth, attracted to anything that shone. Maybe it couldn't see in the dark. But then again he could be totally wrong.

They went down a few steps into the first corridor. They walked slowly, side by side, searching the empty lots with their bright beams, lighting up the spaces behind broken doors. Sebastian was thinking about his books. Would somebody look after them if he didn't come out?

Samir was thinking about Lulu. He'd had to leave her all alone in the flat again, and he wasn't happy about it. Lulu was being weird at the moment. She was restless and excited. In some ways she was on better form than usual. But mostly she was just weird. She kept saying she wanted to get up, even though her skinny legs couldn't support her.

"Samir?" called Lulu.

Nobody answered. She'd been left alone again. Her parents went out most evenings, without telling her, and came back late making lots of noise. But Samir never left her on her own without letting her know. She was sure she hadn't fallen asleep. She'd slept a lot less these last few days. She had loads of energy. She wanted to get up and walk and run and dance.

She'd even given it a go. Yesterday evening she'd managed to lift herself out of bed and take three steps. Then she'd fallen. But she hadn't shouted out or cried. It had taken her at least three hours to climb back onto her mattress. Nobody had noticed.

Her elbows were still sore. So were her hands and knees. But she didn't care. She was determined to try again. She wanted to get up and walk, like other kids. She wanted to run. And dance. What else did kids do? Skip. Play hopscotch. She was convinced she could do it. Maybe she really was getting better. Something had definitely changed over the past few days, and it wasn't her medicine. So what was it?

Lulu moved her legs over the blankets and dangled them into what seemed like a huge void. The floor was so far down, so far away.

But there was a new feeling inside her. A powerful feeling.

The Force.

"I want to walk," she moaned. "I want to. I want to."

She put her hands on the edge of the mattress and pushed herself off, jumping into the big unknown. So far away. So far down.

Together, Sebastian and Samir trained their torches on the pale outline of Prosper the ghost.

"Don't tell me that's all it is!" Sebastian shouted.

"Shh," hissed Samir.

Prosper had never hurt anybody. And Samir knew he hadn't run for his life from a painted ghost. If he'd had any doubts, he could have looked at the floor. He'd left his own bloody trail along the underground corridors.

Sebastian put his bag down. "What's that?"

"What? Oh that... The boiler."

"Is it far now?" he asked nervously.

Samir jerked his chin. "Lot 401."

Sebastian wasn't in any rush to carry on exploring. He put down his torch and unzipped his sports bag. "Hold that!" he whispered, handing the garlic plait to Samir. Samir took it silently and hooked the loop over a jacket button. "You carry it," ordered Sebastian. "I've got the stake."

The piece of wood carved to a point was as long as his bag. He had all the kit to hunt down a vampire. But, judging from Samir's description, it didn't sound anything like a vampire. The creature was more likely to be a ghost or one of the living dead. Which made things a lot more difficult.

Sebastian pushed his classmate in front using the pointy end of the stick. So far, everything had gone according to plan. They went past the boiler and into the corridor that led to door 401.

Samir was taking very small steps now. He kept looking over his shoulder, as if he was frightened Sebastian might try to slip away unnoticed. The beam of light from his torch was directed towards the floor, but it was shaky because his hand kept trembling.

All of a sudden he raised his torch and let out a cry of horror. "Somebody's there!"

The two boys froze, shining their torches on the body slumped against the basement wall.

"D'you think he's…?" stammered Sebastian.

"Looks like it."

"Let's get out of here."

Samir decided to take a closer look. He lit up the man's lifeless face. The corpse's skin was blackened in places, and tattered clothes were stuck to his flesh. He shuddered.

"Let's get out of here," Sebastian urged again.

But the broken door to lot 401 was so close now.

"Nearly there," said Samir, trying to bolster their morale. Something caught his eye. Something on the ground, near the mystery man's open hand. A wallet? Samir bent down and slipped it into his pocket without looking at it. It was hard, with an antenna. He could feel what it was. A mobile phone. Maybe the man had tried to call for help.

"What are you doing?" Sebastian asked him. *What am I doing, for that matter?* Crazy thoughts were flying round inside his head. *Samir had lured him into a trap. Samir had killed somebody. Samir wanted to pin the crime on him. I've got to get out of here fast,* he thought. But his classmate grabbed him by the sleeve. When Sebastian saw Samir's twisted expression, he understood how real his fear of the ghost was.

They were in front of the broken-down door to lot 401. Instinctively they pressed their torches to their bodies, to give off as little light as possible.

"There it is," whispered Samir.

"What?"

"The box."

Samir's cousins had said there was two grand's worth of gear inside it. Screwing up his eyes, Sebastian could just make it out in the gloom. Only seven or eight metres away. Pick it up. And run. Easy enough. But he couldn't resist turning round. He could have sworn the corpse had moved.

Samir put his torch down. "I'm going in. Can you give me some light? Just a bit."

It couldn't have been easier.

Samir picked his way through the damp shadows. Behind him, Sebastian let go of the stake to light Samir's path, filtering the beam between his fingers.

Samir bent down. He grabbed hold of the large flat box. And stood up.

But it was already too late.

The monster was waiting for him in the gloom.

Samir dropped the box. He couldn't believe it. Why hadn't he seen it before? He knew why: the creature had changed. It hardly shone at all now. It had been swamped in darkness right up until the last moment. And now here it was standing in front of him, pale, hazy, expressionless. Like a half-melted snowman.

The garlic.

Samir pulled a button off his jacket as he tugged at the plait. He threw the garlic at the monster, which was hovering restlessly in the dark.

No. It wasn't a vampire.

"Out of the way!"

Sebastian's voice seemed to be calling out to him from the end of a very long tunnel. Samir shuffled backwards, twisted his ankle and collapsed painfully onto the coal heap. He saw the stake flying past his nose. Sebastian had hurled it with all his might.

But the monster of Hummingbird Tower wasn't scared of garlic or stakes.

Still, the attack did provoke a reaction. The creature sprayed blue sparks and turned to face Sebastian.

Samir used the opportunity to crawl out of reach. Sebastian thought he'd be able to escape – he reckoned both of them could make a getaway. He could hardly believe his eyes when he realized Samir wasn't giving up on his precious box. There he was, waiting to pounce on it.

Sebastian put his torch face down on the floor, to muffle the light, and dived with both hands into the open sports bag. He grabbed everything he could lay his hands on. The three stones he threw at the creature didn't do much. Then...

To his horror, he saw the torch topple over and roll on the ground. The ray of light caught the monster, apparently giving it a sudden surge of energy. He held out an old yellowing copy of the Bible in his right hand. In his left was a golden crucifix.

Nothing doing. The monster clearly didn't believe in God or Satan.

Sebastian didn't know if it was a vampire, a ghost, a werewolf or a member of the living dead, but he knew it was about to grab him in its flashing arms. He rummaged in his bag for the last time.

Nothing left.

Hold on. He could feel something in one of the corners. A toy. A transparent plastic revolver. That morning, Sebastian had gone to St Guinevere's Church in the old part of Moreland Town and secretly filled the gun with holy water.

"No!" he shouted as he saw the monster heading towards him.

He pulled the trigger. Even though the gun was silly and made of plastic.

The little trickle of holy water sprayed the darkness. It came into contact with the abominable creature. Both Samir and Sebastian thought a fuse had blown. But actually it was inside their heads. They felt as if they'd stuck their fingers into an electric socket.

She'd done it! Lulu had managed to get her feet to touch the floor and her legs had supported her. She'd stayed there for a while, clutching the brass ball on top of her bedpost. Eventually she let go and started walking. One step … two steps … three steps. All the way to the window.

The tarmac stretched before her eyes. It had been a long time, a very long time since Lulu had last seen the sleepy tower blocks, the balconies with all the washing hung out to dry, the cars parked along the kerbs. Most of all, it'd been a long time since she'd seen the moon.

Her knuckles were white from gripping the window ledge. But she held on. Nothing would ever get in the way of her walking again. Maybe she'd make it as far as the kitchen tomorrow.

The thunderstorm swooped down. A flash of lightning lit up the windows and shook her from head to toe. Lulu let go.

When she came to, she was stretched out on the cold floor and her heart was beating fit to burst. Her body was on fire.

"Samir!" she called. "Samir!"

Samir was in danger. Lulu was sure of it.

It had been a terrible shock. Sitting opposite each other on the floor, the two boys looked dazed.

There was no trace of the monster.

"The holy water," whispered Sebastian.

Samir didn't know anything about any water, but he swore he'd always carry a flask of it in his pocket from now on. He was the first to pull himself together. "Quick!" he shouted.

He stood up, nearly forgetting…

"The box!" He went to pick it up, peering anxiously into the shadows. But nothing moved.

The two boys left lot 401. They passed silently in front of the body slumped against the wall. Their wobbly legs got them as far as the boiler, as far as Prosper, as far as the last few steps.

It had turned into a balmy night. Sebastian looked gratefully up at the moon. He wanted to hold it in his arms and kiss it. "What about him?" he asked.

"Who?"

"The dead guy. What are we going to do about him?"

Samir shrugged. "Er … nothing."

"Don't you think we should tell the police?"

Samir suddenly remembered the small item he'd slipped into his pocket. "Are you mad? D'you want them to think we did him in?"

"I wonder how he died?" Sebastian shuddered.

"If you ask me, he didn't have any holy water."

"The rats'll eat him. We can't leave him there!"

"You do what you like," Samir told Sebastian. "I never saw him."

"I'll take care of it."

Sebastian didn't get a wink of sleep all night. Every time his eyelids felt heavy, he thought he saw a white electrically charged blob appearing before him.

Early the next morning, he walked to a phone box. When he asked to speak to the police, he held a hanky over his mouth and imitated Homer Simpson from *The Simpsons*. A drowsy voice answered him, and Sebastian broke the news.

"There's a dead body in the basements of Hummingbird Tower."

He hung up and laughed nervously, because what he'd just said sounded so stupid. Then he went to school. And, for the first time in his life, he failed a geography test.

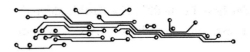

Golem and Farting Goo

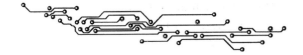

Hugh started emptying the basket his mother had left on the kitchen table. Big B cola, Mega B pizza, Special B cereal. You didn't have to be a genius to work out where Mrs Mullins had been shopping. At the bottom of the basket he also found a large quantity of a less edible purchase. Something he was familiar with because he'd confiscated it from Miguel so many times. Big B farting goo.

He went into the sitting room to ask his mother a question or two. But Mrs Mullins was in no mood to answer.

"I spent all afternoon battling with your computer!" she shouted. "It's driving me mad."

"That's because you don't know how to use it properly."

Hugh's mother preferred to write by hand. But when she was submitting an article to a magazine, she needed to use the computer. Mrs Mullins contributed to *Psychology: Keys to the Mind*, and debated such stimulating topics as "The Art of Conversation in Lifts" and "Should We Knock Down the Tower Blocks on Our Estates?"

"Golem, schmolem!" she moaned. "I've had it up to here with that thing!"

Hugh was dumbstruck. "You've been playing?" he asked, after a long pause.

"Of course not! I'm much too old for those kinds of games," she exclaimed, giving her son a withering look, as if to say, *And so are you, my poor boy.* "I just wanted to type up my article in peace. Not a chance. I couldn't concentrate with that ridiculous ghost wandering all over the screen. It's horrible! You feel like it's after you."

Hugh laughed. "Yeah, Joke can get a bit much sometimes."

"Joke? Is that what you call it? Can't you get rid of it?"

Hugh shook his head. "Er ... no. It's some kind of virus."

"The pizza!" exclaimed his mother, getting up quickly. "I forgot to put it in the freezer."

Hugh followed her into the kitchen. "What's all this about?" he asked, pointing to the tubs of Big B farting goo.

"That? Er ... I don't know. It was on special offer," she stammered. "I thought ... you might like some."

Hugh tried to come up with a smart one-liner. He was particularly embarrassed because, although he'd never admit it, he'd kept three tubs of the goo he'd confiscated. "It's not going to be the subject of your next article for *Psychology*, is it?" he asked.

His mother was unperturbed. "Now, there's an idea!" she exclaimed. "And I think I've even got a title: 'Golem and Farting Goo: The Kids Who Never Grow Up'."

"I'll go and lay the table," Hugh said grumpily.

Samir unscrewed the cap and squirted some white cream from the tube into his hand. "It's what the chemist recommended," he told Lulu.

The little girl had strange scorch marks on her arms and tummy. She'd had them when Samir returned from his eventful trip to the basements with Sebastian and found her lying at the foot of her bed, delirious.

He rubbed on the cream. "That's better. It doesn't look so red now."

Lulu shook her little head on the pillow. "No," she complained, "it's not any better."

"Of course it is."

"No. It's gone."

"What's gone?"

"The Force."

Samir shrugged. "You'll never be strong. You've just got to get used to it."

"No," said Lulu, putting him straight. "I'm not talking about just being strong. I'm talking about the Force."

"You think you're in *Star Wars* or something?"

"You just don't get it."

"The best thing you can get is some sleep."

Lulu shut her eyes obediently. But she added, "When it's here, I can walk."

"Whatever."

Samir tiptoed out, closing the bedroom door. Lulu wasn't his only worry.

The police had turned up at Hummingbird Tower that morning. They'd found the body. In theory, Samir had nothing to worry about, since there hadn't been any witnesses to their nocturnal adventure. But would Sebastian keep his mouth shut?

As for his cousins, it wouldn't take them long to make the link. And then what would they do? They'd got their gear and that was all they were interested in, Samir kept telling himself. They were hardly going to believe that ... what? That Samir had bumped off some guy who'd got in the way when he was trying get their box back?

He took the mobile phone out of his pocket. It was a good-looking model, worth a lot. The weirdest thing was, it was still charged up. Samir could have used it. But he didn't dare. Something warned him it'd be dangerous. He tried to see what make it was. But he couldn't find anything apart from a tiny logo. BIT in a circle intersected by meridians, as the geography teacher would have put it, representing planet earth. It didn't mean anything to him. Probably some foreign brand. But the more he thought about it, the more he was convinced he'd already seen that BIT logo stamped across a globe somewhere before.

Back at the Badachs', it was lesson time. Majid had turned into his mum's teacher. Emmay could recognize simple words at first glance now. But unfortunately most words are complicated. Sitting next to Majid, she was staring helplessly at the screen.

"All iz same?" she asked, astonished.

Majid confirmed that *won, fun, done, son* and *sun* were all pronounced the same way.

"Like *one*?" she asked, sticking a thumb up.

"Yes."

Majid was making progress too. At the same time as he was teaching the words to his mum, he was learning how to spell them properly.

"Iz more worse than *iz* and *hiz*." Emmay declared. She pursed her lips and added, "They do it on purpose, to make language more difficult for foreeners."

"No, even Sebastian makes mistakes—" Majid

stopped, baffled by the rude noise Emmay had just made. "OK, shall we carry on?" he asked. He did a double take. She'd just done it again.

"Iz 'orrible!" she exclaimed. She threw the little ball she'd been holding in her left hand onto the table.

"What are you doing?"

"Iz farting goo," she said, scrunching up her nose.

"Emmay? Are you all right?"

Majid's mum looked surprised to see the goo, as if she didn't know how it had got there. "They iz doing special offer, Majid. And I buy farting goo. Iz special offer for you, innit?"

Majid creased up with laughter. Deep down he was chuffed. He'd been wanting to buy some goo for a while now.

"They got you, oh yes, they did!"

"Majid! Stop! Stop right now!"

"Is there a law against laughing?"

But his mum wasn't thinking about farting goo any more. She was looking darkly at the screen.

Golem had just appeared in big letters. The game was back. The game was calling him.

"Emmay! I've earned it!" he begged. "It's so unfair!"

"Not yet, Majid, not yet."

He knew that when the game installed itself like that, you could only get rid of it by shutting everything down and rebooting the computer. Reluctantly Majid pressed the reset button.

He had a brand-new keyboard from Hugh. He had the latest printer, left behind by the Shrinkers. He had the only computer of its kind on the estate, a New Generation BIT computer, with BIT superimposed across a picture of the globe. But he couldn't use it.

And all this time, Calimero was flirting with Natasha. Come to think of it, why didn't he pay his English teacher a visit?

So that Saturday, Calimero and Magic Berber were sitting side by side in front of Hugh's computer. They'd been exploring Golemia, where Natasha was queen, for nearly an hour. When Majid got up to yawn and have a stretch, he noticed a whole series of small tubs on the shelf.

"It's catching, that stuff!"

"Sorry?"

Majid pointed to the Big B farting goo. "You confiscated it," he guessed.

"Yes, from my mother."

Majid took a minute to digest this information. "Special offers are a real problem for mums," he concluded.

He telephoned Emmay a bit before seven to tell her he'd be home late. He wasn't sure she swallowed his story of a private lesson with Mr Mullins, but anyway...

At eight they tucked into some sandwiches. They'd spent a long time riding Bubble the dragon through Golemia's labyrinths, collecting life points here, and pieces of gold you could buy special powers with there. Now they were admiring Natasha.

"Have you bought her any special powers yet?"

"She can clear one metre eighty in the high jump, and she runs the hundred metres in twelve seconds dead," joked Hugh.

"Don't tell me you've made her into a sports freak?"

"She's young and she needs a career. I thought she could be a PE teacher..."

Majid rolled his eyes. "Natasha could be anything in the world, and what d'you go and do? It's like Allah not creating the sea and the stars, but making ... the Moreland Estate instead!"

"OK, OK," Hugh conceded. "I did also think I'd grant her the power of invisibility. What d'you reckon?"

"When you're as fit as she is? Seems like a waste to me."

After a heated debate, they decided Natasha would be warm-hearted but not a pushover; intelligent but not pretentious; sporty but not a PE teacher; she'd be interested in films, reading and cars; she'd never buy farting goo; she'd be a good cook; and she wouldn't want kids yet.

As far as special powers went, it was agreed that she would stay visible (ideally she could be duplicated) but she'd be able to see in the dark. And while they were at it, she'd be able to breathe underwater too.

"I'm not sure the program can handle all that," Hugh objected, returning to planet earth for a moment.

"Look," Majid whispered.

Natasha had turned towards them, holding out her hands with a smile that would melt an iceberg.

"She looks like she wants to join us."

Hugh couldn't help agreeing. He clicked on the screen, suddenly impatient to carry on with the game. But he'd clicked without noticing that the little arrow was flashing over a large wooden door at the back of the room.

Instantly the door opened.

And they came flooding in.

A horde, an angry mob. As if they'd all been waiting.

"Natasha!" Hugh shouted.

"Fight, you've got to defend yourself!" Majid yelled.

No two monsters were the same. A devil with a forked tail, a hysterical dwarf, a slithering grub, a Cyclops with a beaming face, a headless knight, a witch with black nails, a snake with feet, a frog with a giraffe's neck, disembodied jaws, something slimy ... they just kept coming and coming. They were all rushing towards Natasha.

"Fight back!" urged Majid, stamping his feet impatiently. "Trip them up!"

Hugh finally reacted. He pressed key after key –
1, 6, right arrow, left arrow. Flames billowed in
every direction. He made the little warrior pierce,
hack and decapitate.

"Bubble, help!" called Calimero desperately.

The dragon cleared one whole corner of the
room with his blazing breath, reducing ten attack-
ers to ashes.

But the door was still open. Fresh waves of
monsters kept surging in, drowning everything.
The little warrior, the dragon. And Natasha.

She was struggling to defend herself, flexing her
arms. Soon all you could see was her pretty blonde
head. Her beautiful green eyes were filled with terror. It made for depressing viewing. Then, abruptly,
the screen froze.

Game over appeared in big letters, followed by
the ritual commands:

➤ start play
➤ end play

"Start again," Majid whispered.

Hugh looked devastated. The sweat was pouring
down his face. It occurred to Majid that some of

the drops glistening on his cheeks might actually be tears.

"Go home, Majid. It's over for today."

"You're not going to give up? You've got to make her all over again. You've got to create Natasha again."

"Yeah, yeah," choked Hugh. "And from now on I'll know. The door. Close the door."

Majid went back to Hummingbird Tower. Before going up to his flat, he thought about the body that'd been found in the basements. He had a strong urge to go down there, to push open the door to the basements. But opening doors didn't seem such a great idea this evening.

Just then, he heard a whining noise coming from the bowels of the earth. He rushed towards the main staircase and climbed the steps four at a time.

His flat was dark and quiet. His dad had already come home, eaten his supper and gone to bed. Majid felt cheated. That idiot Calimero had wrecked everything. He wasn't up to the job of protecting Natasha. What a stupid idea, making a girl-golem. In Golem City, which was Magic Berber's universe, that kind of thing would never have happened. He'd have created a superhero who could defend himself. He definitely had to continue with the game. Who knew where it'd lead him?

He took off his shoes in the middle of the living room. He didn't feel like going to bed yet. What was stopping him from playing now, while everybody was asleep? He detected a slight noise. Like the sound of gentle snoring. He felt strangely uneasy as he scanned the shadowy room.

Suddenly he saw a green eye light up, right there in front of him. The noise was getting louder. It only lasted for a few seconds. Then stopped. And he realized what was happening. The printer had just switched itself on.

Shakily he made his way over to the computer. A sheet of white paper had emerged, glistening, from the printer. Majid grabbed it with a sweaty hand. He went to the window to get a better look in the moonlight. And read:

**Play, Magic Berber, play.
I'm waiting for you.**

WHAT will happen if Magic Berber and
Calimero keep playing Golem?

WHO is the monster haunting the basements
of Hummingbird Tower?

WHY do the delivery men from Price Shrinkers
want Majid's computer back?

Find out in the next episode of Golem:

Joke

Turn the page to read Chapter 1...

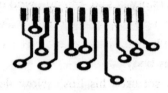

Where's Chechnya?

The small van was hurtling towards the Moreland Estate. Inside it were a journalist and her cameraman. There was no time to waste. They had to file the report by 8 p.m.

"Aren't people fed up with stories about mashed-up estates?" asked Momo the cameraman. "There was one last week about joyriders in Rokaz. And yesterday it was kids staging a hold-up in a grocery store in Fester—"

Emily Barter cut him short. "Compared with Chechnya, this is a holiday."

"Yeah, well, when you look at it that way," he said grudgingly. "So, what's the story?"

"The police received an anonymous phone call about a body in the basements of Hummingbird Tower on the Moreland Estate. They followed up the lead, and that's exactly what they found. But there was no ID."

"Usual story," said Momo, who'd seen everything after twenty years of filming news reports.

"But it hots up because the guy had burn marks all over his body."

Momo smacked his lips. "Now *that's* more like it. Are we talking torture in the basements? Kids killing time? We'll have to find out if the residents heard any cries for help." He was hungry for a scoop. They'd grill the losers in this dump and land themselves an exclusive. *They heard him screaming in the night. Now they're afraid to leave their homes. Who will be next?*

He started whistling. They might even get the headline slot. The newsreader would look directly into the camera and say darkly: "Spring's in the air, but there's panic on the streets."

When he saw the grey concrete towers of the Moreland Estate sticking up against the sky, Momo scowled. Not very photogenic. He slowed down level with two boys playing football. "Hey, guys! Which is Hummingbird Tower?"

The older boy came over to the van. "It's the TV!" he shouted to his younger brother. "Have you come about the murder?"

"Got it in one," said Momo. "So where's this Hummingbird Tower?"

"Can we have your autograph?" asked the older brother.

"*He's* not famous," scoffed the younger one. "You ever seen him on TV?"

The cameraman tapped the steering wheel. Some people around here needed a kick up the backside. "Are you going to tell me or not?"

The older brother explained at great length. "On the right, see the second building over there? Well, it's not that one. You take a left."

Momo frowned as he repeated the instructions, then set off without bothering to thank them. The kids waited for the van to disappear before knocking their fists together. "Touch, blud!"

They'd sent Momo in the wrong direction.

Fifteen minutes later, the van was back.

"This place is starting to get on my nerves," Momo complained. "If I land on those kids again…"

"They didn't just lose us in Chechnya," Emily reminded him, "they kidnapped us into the bargain."

"Yeah, well, when you look at it that way," he grunted. "Hold on a minute, let's ask Grandad over there… 'Scuse me!"

Grandad dragged his wolfhound over to the van. He was suspicious at first but soon broke into a broad smile. The TV!

"We're looking for Hummingbird Tower."

"Well, you've come to the right person," said Grandad. "I'm the caretaker."

Emily and Momo glanced at each other. They wanted Grandad on camera.

"Would you mind if we asked you a few questions?" said the journalist.

"Don't I have to be made up for the TV?"

Emily nearly laughed in the old man's face. "No, we don't bother for the news."

They decided to set up in front of Hummingbird Tower. Momo lifted the camera onto his shoulder while Emily started the interview.

"You're the caretaker of Hummingbird Tower. Did you ever think a murder would happen here?"

"To be honest with you," the caretaker replied, "anything could happen round here. Just take Brutus."

"Who?"

"My dog."

Momo re-angled the camera to film the wolfhound.

"He had a funny turn on the night of the murder," said Grandad. "He always pees just here on this bollard, opposite the main entrance" – we're going to have to edit that bit out, thought Emily – "but he was edgy that evening. Growling, his eyes rolling... Strange that, because he's regular as clockwork is our Brutus. Always pees bang on time, on the bollard—"

"Fine," Emily interrupted. "But what about you? Did you notice anything suspicious that night?"

"To be honest with you, there's been all these power cuts. The lift keeps breaking down, the bulbs keep going. Twenty years I've been caretaker here. Never seen anything like it. You put in a brand-new bulb and pop, it goes just like that!"

Momo sighed and lowered the camera. Grandad was a basket case. Ask him about a murder and he started talking about the national grid.

Just then a pretty West African girl walked out of Hummingbird Tower.

"Hey!" Momo called out.

Aisha went up to them shyly.

"D'you live in this building?" asked Emily. "Would you mind answering a few questions?"

"It's for the TV," Momo added, as if he was trying to bribe a toddler with a bag of sweets.

"I don't know if I'm allowed to," Aisha stammered. She'd been brought up strictly and her dad might blast her for talking to a stranger. Then again, it was for TV...

Emily started the interview regardless. Momo resumed filming.

"So you live in Hummingbird Tower. Did you know a dead body's been found in the basements? Have you noticed anything suspicious lately?"

"Yes," answered Aisha, looking away. "There's smoke floating around on my landing. And it sends out sparks."

Momo groaned and put the camera down again.

"Wait, we might be on to something," said Emily. "Where do you think this smoke is coming from? Are there kids messing about with fire?"

"No!" Aisha panicked. "No way! It's smoke without fire. It's the spirits of dead people coming back to visit us."

"They're all basket cases here!" declared Momo, switching off his camera.

"Let's try one more," sighed Emily.